Slocum blinked his ⟨...⟩
out of the treeline ⟨...⟩
They were shooting at him—puffs of gun smoke were swept away by the wind. Whoever was cutting all the caps at Black Wolf meant business. Then he saw Black Wolf go down in the snow; they'd shot him. Slocum spurred his horse at them with his own Colt in hand. The three figures began to blast away at him. The range was too far and he held his own fire. He decided they couldn't hit a bull in the ass and would soon be out of ammo.

"Jacks, you one-eyed bastard!" he shouted when he recognized the ringleader. "You better throw your hands up! Or I'm coming to kill you!"

He took aim off the plunging deck of his pony. In sync with the horse's rocking gait, he sent his first shot . . .

JAKE LOGAN

SLOCUM AND THE
NEBRASKA STORM

JOVE BOOKS, NEW YORK

SLOCUM AND THE NEBRASKA STORM

A Jove Book / published by arrangement with
the author

PRINTING HISTORY
Jove edition / March 2000

All rights reserved.
Copyright © 2000 by Penguin Putnam Inc.
This book may not be reproduced in whole or in part,
by mimeograph or any other means, without permission.
For information address: The Berkley Publishing Group,
a division of Penguin Putnam Inc.,
375 Hudson Street, New York, New York 10014.

The Penguin Putnam Inc. World Wide Web site address is
http://www.penguinputnam.com

ISBN: 0-515-12769-8

A JOVE BOOK®
Jove Books are published by The Berkley Publishing Group,
a division of Penguin Putnam Inc.,
375 Hudson Street, New York, New York 10014.
JOVE and the "J" design
are trademarks belonging to Penguin Putnam Inc.

PRINTED IN THE UNITED STATES OF AMERICA

10 9 8 7 6 5 4 3 2 1

1

The north wind singed his whisker-bristled jaw. Its arctic force seared his watery eyes and blurred his vision of the snow-blanketed land ahead. Grey woolly clouds shut off the weak sunshine. He raised the reins and booted the hesitant horse onward through the knee-deep drifts. His inability, in the storm's fury, to make out the long pine ridge that he knew lay five or six miles to his right added to his concern. From deep in his chest, a hacking cough erupted that threatened to cut off his air. When at last the choking cough trailed away, he wiped his runny nose on a rag from his coat, then with his gloved hand jammed the rag back in his side pocket. This miserable head cold was going to kill him yet.

He couldn't be over a mile or so from Jim Bordeaux's trading post. The trouble was it was only a dugout in this vastness, and he might ride right past it. He searched for the smoke from the fireplace to find its location. However, with the fierce wind, there wouldn't be much of a sign of anything before it was swept away in the snow that swirled around him. Despite the three-point blanket wrapped over his long canvas coat, he still shivered with a fever. He was too numb to think, and he needed to find Bordeaux's and not get lost out in these blizzard conditions. There might be more snow coming on the wings of this new blast. A man could expect anything in the Nebraska Panhandle this time of year.

He reached up and pulled down the brim of his wool Scotch cap. It was a far cry from the usual broad-brimmed felt hat he'd worn the preceding fall up from Texas ramrodding the outfit that delivered Chester Thomas's herd of longhorns. Nonetheless, his head felt warm and his ears under the flaps weren't frozen—yet. A man had to be some kind of a real fool to have stayed up in this polar waste when the warm cantinas in south Texas rang every night with the soft melodious music of castanets, guitars, and fiddles. There were silky-dressed olive-skinned girls to flirt and dance with a man until the sun came up. He could hear the trumpet of the band— no, it was only the whistle of the unrelenting wind,

If he rode past Bordeaux's post and didn't find it, he would damn sure freeze to death in this wasteland. In a few hours it would be dark. After that he'd be wolf bait. There was nothing to kick up and burn out here, that was for certain.

He could visualize the sway of Juanita's hips under the red skirt, the clack of castanets in her long fingers keeping time to her stomping feet. The hem of her skirt raised high enough to show off her shapely olive-colored calves. Her heels marking the beat across the flat rock floor in Antonio's. Evil glinting in her dark eyes, calling out not for some meek male to fumble around in a limp attempt to conquer her flesh, but for a real man, a stallion, to take her lusty voluptuous body.

Slocum's coughing again brought him back to reality. The knife of the cold air in his desperate lungs blurred his vision and a depleting weakness consumed his entire body. He couldn't fight much in this condition. Good thing for him he wasn't so weak with this cold when he'd had that fight for his life. He never could have wrestled with an Indian buck for the one skinning knife on the ground during their hand-to-hand confrontation. They'd called him Blue Elk. Slocum didn't know his name at the time, but he heard his rude claim that the buffalo Slocum worked to skin was his own. Blue Elk jumped off his horse, proclaiming ownership of the carcass, and made a charge. Slocum brushed his attack aside, then watched the powerfully built Sioux spring to his feet. He came right back and they became locked in a fierce hand-to-hand struggle that matched two equally well-muscled men in combat. They rolled and twisted on the ground, Slocum's seeking a superior position over the others.

The knife Slocum started to skin the animal with became the goal of both men. Elk tried to reach for it and Slocum knew he would have to kill him, if the angry Sioux ever grasped the handle. No longer were their effects the wrestling-match of two men pitted to physically defeat the other—this combat had reached life-and-death proportions.

Slocum grew aware of others—their fighting had drawn a crowd of onlookers. Their cheers of encouragement and "ohs" were vocal and sounded very Indian. They were no doubt an audience of his adversary's kind and he wondered if any of them would come to the aid of their red brother. But so far, him grappling alone with the big buck must have satisfied them.

At last Elk's hand reached the knife's thick wooden handle. Like a cat, he sprang up with it, slashed the air with the blade, and the war cry came from deep in his throat. A death call; Slocum rolled aside and in the process kicked Elk hard enough in the leg to stagger the man.

In a bound, Slocum was on his feet. He ducked in, grasped Elk's knife hand, swung it behind his back, and drove the warrior to his knees. The knife clattered to the ground and Slocum shoved the man's face down into the dry buffalo grass. With wooden handle in his left hand, he held the keen blade at the side of Elk's neck. Then silence. Slocum looked up at the sober faces of the warriors surrounding him, each seated on a brightly painted buffalo horse. . . .

Now his coughing cut off his breathing and threatened to draw his testicles up into his belly. His eyes and nose both ran at the same time. He blew his nose in the icy-cold rag. Where in the hell was the trading post? He twisted in the saddle and tried to look back for any signs. Had he ridden past it? Only the bitter wind answered his silent question.

His horse snorted, then lifted his head to catch a sound on the whistling wind. Slocum heard some other horses whinny. His cow pony had found them, thank God. Slocum drew a deep breath and prayed he didn't have to cough again. On the brink of a creek, he saw them below him, the snow-frosted animals munching on hay. To his left stood the familiar low structure, a dugout cut back in the slope with only the log front exposed. It served Bordeaux as a storehouse. Further on, the main structure was notched into the hillside. A candle's light shone like a friendly beacon through the six-pane window.

He dismounted heavily on the frozen crust that gave under his boot soles. His legs were slow to stiffen enough to support him, and he clung with both hands to the saddlehorn. His nose ran worse, and his eyes burned with tears.

"Come inside," the heavily accented Frenchman called out from the doorway. Wrapped in a buffalo-robe coat, he hurried over.

"Got to put my horse up," Slocum said weakly.

"Aye, you sound bad. Best you go inside and warm up," the burly man said, and took his horse. "I will feed him and put the saddle and gear in the lean-to, no?"

"Thanks—"

"Slocum, that is you? Holy Saint Maria, you look bad, man. Go inside. My Jeanne will care for you. You are sick, no?"

Slocum was too exhausted to argue with the man. He took the heavy Winchester from the scabbard and then with much effort, drew his head up to try to clear it. Bits of ice stung his face as he coughed his way to the front door. Inside at last, out of breath, he pressed his back to the rough-hewn cottonwood logs.

A tall, handsome woman with her dark black hair in braids rushed to help him. Her beauty warmed him, and he knew he'd made the right decision to come to the trading post for help.

"Slocum?" she cried when she recognized the man standing at the wall.

"I'll be fine," he said, and tried to wave aside her concern. The warmth of the room made the frozen skin on his face and nose seem to burn. Safe at last, he sighed, out of breath, and his knees threatened to buckle. Jeanne took the Winchester from him, then moved under his arm to lead him to the large bed in the corner of the great room.

"I'm too dirty to lie on your bed," he mumbled in protest.

"Nonsense, you must lay down. You may already have pneumonia. What are you doing out in such weather anyway with such a cold?"

He blinked his watery eyes at her, then drew a quick breath. "Coming here—so you could cure me."

"My God, man, why did you wait so long?" She eased him down on the bed, stripping his icy-stiff blanket wrap away, then covering him again with one of her own.

"Didn't know—" His deep coughing consumed him and he half rose to hack over the edge of the mattress, afraid he might drown in his own phlegm. "Didn't know it would—" He paused for his breath. "Get this damn bad."

"Lie down. I have some salve that might help you." She gave him a look of disapproval before she ran off after her medicine. He settled back to stare at the underside of the roof's shingles. A cold shiver ran up his spine and his entire body shook despite the warmth from the blazing fireplace in the other corner. Maybe she could cure him. He hoped so, and closed his sore eyes. His conscience nagged at him for lying on her clean quilts in his filthy clothes.

He fell asleep for a moment. When he opened his eyes, she forced a spoonful of coal oil and brown sugar into his mouth. Like the burst of a bomb, it rushed through his constricted throat in a flash of fire. But shortly, he began to breathe easier.

"You need some willow-bark tea," she said.

He could barely see her through his blurred vision. Tears streamed off his face in rivers. Tea sounded better than her harsh dosage of medicine. The coal-oil fumes scorched his sore nostrils, and he could still taste the sharp oiliness on his tongue.

"My goodness, you are close to dying," she declared and went off to her fireplace.

The entire room was walled in with square-cut hand-hewed log sides, three quarters of it wedged into the deep cut in the bank. The exposed side faced south and looked like a regular cabin on the outside. The far end of the long room was the trading post with a counter and goods for sale. This end was their living quarters, with a fireplace, table, chairs, and the great bed with ropes to support the tick mattress under him.

A tall wooden headboard rose above his head. He could lie back and study the lamp's shadows in the rafters and the underside of the shingle roof that was covered with dirt on top.

"You have a bad cold?" Bordeaux said, bringing a chair across to sit beside him.

"Yeah, thought I'd get over it, but it got worse." Slocum rose on his elbow and blew his nose. In the cherry light of the fireplace he could see Jeanne squatted down to swing the kettle over the flames in the hearth.

"He is a sick man," she said, and shook her head in dismay.

"Ah, you will get him well." Bordeaux laughed aloud, then turned to grin at Slocum. "Ah, *oui*, you must get him well, my dear. I need to hire him to go take my furs to Independence and bring back the goods I have ordered."

"This time of year?" Slocum squinted his eyes in disbelief at the man.

"Ah, it will soon be spring up here. The time to leave is soon so you can get back when the Sioux bring in the prime hides."

"It isn't spring yet." In dismay, Slocum shook his head at the man's plans. All he needed was to be outside, freezing his butt off and trying to get to Independence with a pack train. No, thanks.

"Don't worry him with such nonsense." Jeanne elbowed her husband aside with a look of impatience. "He is far too sick to send anywhere."

In her long fingers she cradled a steaming cup. With a knee on the bed, she let him work himself up to a sitting position, then held the cup to his lips. The metal rim burned his skin at first touch, but the liquid slid down his throat and he began to feel the misery in his body evaporate.

He paused to take a troubled breath. "Willow-bark tea?"

"*Oui*, you will feel better in a little while."

He nodded and sipped some more, supporting himself with both arms stiff behind his back. With each swallow, the pain in his throat began to diminish. In his dull daze, he studied the table lamp's flickering light.

"We have company." Bordeaux bolted to his feet. "Sioux."

Through the tea vapors, Slocum watched the big man cross

the floor. The persistent pounding at his temples eased and when he drank the rest of the soothing liquid, he lay back and she tucked him in. He knew in a moment the scratching in his throat would erupt into hard coughing, and fought the urge— until the Sioux left anyway. But to no avail.

2

Black Wolf sat cross-legged on buffalo skins. Wind tore at the side walls of the tepee and wailed across the land. The glowing fire in the circle of rock gave off the pungent smell of sage. It burned hotter and longer than pine or cottonwood. From the sacred smoke that smarted his eyes, he sought to bring up a vision, a dream to guide him. Hard as he tried, nothing appeared, only his own thoughts of the bitter winter outside and the plight of his people.

His oldest wife, Owl Woman, handed him a bowl of stew. She knelt beside him, a worried look on her face. Without speaking, she shared his concerns for the future of the twenty-two lodges. The two of them never needed words spoken aloud. He recalled her as the proud girl of twenty winters before. That spring, he became a warrior and returned to camp with many Crow ponies on his lead rope. They were all colors, painted ponies, and they danced on their toes.

He saw her watch him enter the camp back then. She must be impressed by my horse-thief ways, he decided. Later, after the stories were told in the council of the men, the celebration food eaten and the spirits thanked, he went for a walk.

"You are not as pretty as you think, Wolf Boy," she said from the shadows.

"I am not a boy. I am Black Wolf and someday I will be the chief of all the Sioux." He waited in the starlight, knowing she was standing back in the willows. If he acted too brazen she might run away. He wanted badly to stick his manhood into this maiden. He had experienced such a union several times before with a divorced woman in her tepee—and even with a Crow girl on his last raid. He had captured and used her scrawny body until he tired of her, then gave her to his friends to use. But none of the others he laid with would be like Owl Woman. She was as tall as he was. Her firm breasts jiggled under the deer-hide blouse when she went past him. He had even seen her sleek body when she emerged naked and wet from swimming in the Rose Bud. He had not stared long at her for that was impolite, but he saw enough of her shapely body to know she would be powerful underneath his muscle-corded belly.

Even back then he had visions and knew from them that Owl Woman would be his wife for all of his life. Other women would come too, but she would be the real one for him.

Then he returned to the moment. The wind whistled outside reminding him of the winter's bitter cold. He could smell the buffalo stew Owl Woman had given him. His saliva began to flow; he wiped clean the bone spoon on his dusty leggings. Perhaps food would bring the magic back. His search for the dream to lead his small band into the future avoided him.

Fifteen warriors were all that remained. The rest were old men, old women, wives and children. To think those little ones might cry at night from an empty belly, made him savor the thick broth. How many in his camp would die before the moon of the new cottonwood leaves? So many to feed, so little game left and the Army telling his people what they could and could not do.

"The right vision will come," she said, and rose with a stiffness he had not noticed before.

He nodded that he heard her and sipped on spoonfuls of the stew. Then he looked across at his three wives busy sewing and tending the fire as if they waited for his next words. Owl Woman, the tallest and oldest. Red Cheeks, the middle one, fully pregnant with her great belly impeding her movement as she sewed and talked softly to the small boy, his son Horse Came. The boy stood by her in his deerskin shirt with his genitals exposed like all children that age. Mother and son exchanged a few words.

Owl Woman rose and took the boy outside so he could pee. Black Wolf's youngest wife, Blue Doe, looked busy with her stitches and bead work. She was preparing him a special blouse for springtime and the hunt. Blue Doe had been the wife of his younger brother Bull Awakes. When he was killed in a buffalo hunt, Black Wolf had married her so she would not be forced out. A thin girl, she worried why the spirits never gave her a son, not with her first man and so far not with Black Wolf. He'd promised her he would double his efforts.

"They say that Sitting Bull hates the Red Coats," Red Cheeks said. "Words come they are even bossier than blue legs are to us."

"I have heard the words from Canada," he said. "Still he better stay in the north. They say there are many large herds of the buffalo left to hunt up there."

He finished his stew and set the bowl down. Owl Woman returned and herded the boy to the side of the tepee with his other two children, his daughters, Snail Goes and Blue Wing.

How many of his babies had gone on to join the spirits? He never liked to think of the diseases, plagues, and troubles heaped on his people by the white invaders. He liked to recall on their first night. Owl Woman's virginal screams when he parted her long silky legs that evening on the Rose Bud and they had become one. It was a night he would never forget. He recalled too, their first stillborn baby, blue as the sky in the midwife's hands when she came from his tipi. The woman's pain-wrinkled face told him all he needed to know when without a word, she turned to bear it away. It never even cried for a first breath. Outside, he had listened, heard the slosh of its emergence, then waited forever by the doorway for the sound of its lungs filled with the spring air and screaming "I am here."

Perhaps these bad times would pass for his people. He rose to his feet and swept up the blanket, his body stiff from so much time spent in meditation. If only the vision had come to him, then he would have felt better. Perhaps it was outside. Maybe the Great Sioux Spirit, the White Buffalo Woman, would return to this land and tell him what he should do next.

Strange, for all of his foresight, he never saw a vision telling him of their dead firstborn. That worried him. Years went by and he saw many things, and told others how to avoid dangers in their lives. The previous winter, it came to him that in the spring he and his people must join all the wild Sioux and their allies on the Sweetwater. He felt good taking his people there. They found much game in the region. Everyone was excited. The days of plenty had returned and they knew there would be a big dance and celebration at this rendezvous of the tribes.

In early summer they set up their lodges at the place the whites called Little Bighorn and joined the thousands of others already camped there. The Cheyennes were in a camp to one side, the Arapahos in another. When his own people were settled, he sought the great medicine man's help. Black Wolf spent days and nights in the tepee of Sitting Bull. He hungered to learn more of the man's ways, how to see the future and do the right thing for his people.

He asked Sitting Bull, were there ever times he could not see ahead? The old man nodded his head and for a long time did not answer him. At last he cleared his throat.

"Sometimes the spirits don't want you to know. If you knew the future and it was very bad, the way ahead, I mean, you might destroy yourself."

"How can you tell them you are stronger than that?"

"The spirits know who they can tell. They know better than you. Maybe you think you are strong—" Bull shook his head slowly. "But you do not know like the spirits do. They know who is weak."

"When I do not receive a sign, is that a signal that I am too weak?"

Bull shook his large head so hard the braids danced on his shoulders. "Spirits will always tell you what is necessary. You must have faith."

"But you have seen this great battle vision and I have been here two moons and seen nothing."

"Have strength. The spirits don't wish to repeat what they say to you. They have told me, there will be a big battle. The

Sioux and our allies, the Cheyenne and the Arapahos will all be victorious near here.

"It will be a hot day and very dry," Bull said ignoring his direct question. "The dust like a curtain will blind you. The gun smoke will eat at your vision too. Then there will be no more shots. Only a few will sing the white man's last song. They too will be silenced."

"Will the white man be banished?" Black Wolf wanted to know. Would this be the end of their enemies forever? Why didn't Sitting Bull answer?

He could hear Sitting Bull breathing from outside, the screams of children playing nearby carried to his ears; racing horses' hooves drummed the ground he sat upon. One thing Black Wolf knew from the days he'd spent with the old man was that he had to have more patience.

"I only see storm clouds to follow the victory here," Sitting Bull said. "Many bolts of lightning will strike us. The swollen rivers will swallow us and our many dead will become the feast of the turkey buzzard. I see many buzzards hopping around with their craws packed so full of carrion. They will be so full, they only pause to eat out the eyeballs of our dead women and children."

"Have you told the others?" Black Wolf's heart pounded in his chest at the notion of such a plight for his people.

"They only wish to hear of a great victory. Will you go out and offer yourself in battle knowing this?"

"I will fight the blue legs as I always have."

"Will you foolishly rush into death's arms?" Sitting Bull demanded.

"No," Black Wolf finally admitted. "I have my people to lead. They need me."

"Good. Then I have not told the wrong man."

The large camp's hunts went well. They dried much meat and pounded it to make pemmican later in the season when the chokecherries ripened. Black Wolf could tell the cherries would weigh down the branches in the Moon of the Ripe Ones. He paused several times to examine the small green fruit on the limbs, each bud swelling like a woman's belly. The thought of their tart sweetness drew the water to his tongue.

But their harvest would not come to him, a vision told him while camped on the river the whites called Little Bighorn.

When he spoke of it to Sitting Bull, the man only gave Black Wolf a grave nod as if the matter burdened him too. After the battle, the relentless soldiers' pursuit kept them from ever returning to harvest the bumper crop.

Now Black Wolf stood in the tepee to clear his head, the blanket over his shoulder. He tried to shake away the bitterness of his people's fate after the great battle. He could not dwell in the past; the uncertain future loomed ahead. Maybe even starvation—the strong wind tearing at the buffalo-skin walls reminded him of that possibility too.

"I will go to the trading post," he said. "Perhaps Bordeaux has heard of the repeating rifles he says will come."

"Be careful of the might of the winter wind. It has a strong fist out there," Owl Woman told him.

He nodded. A man must respect the cold, the way a boy growing up must respect his elders. To forget that lesson could cost him his life, not just a switching or strapping. Outside he straightened as daggers of ice on the sharp wind struck his cheek. He took his single-shot .40/60 in the leather scabbard from beside the flap. His weapon did not need the heat or moisture of the tepee to make it sweat the way a man did inside a lodge.

The great paint horse nickered to him. His favorite buffalo horse and three others were held in the corral and fed cottonwood bark and willow shoots. The rest of his band's many horses were turned out to fend for themselves. They were tough stock and could paw through the snow's crust and find the summer's cured grass. Some weak ones would fall to the relentless hungry wolves, but there were plenty of good horses that would survive. When the Moon of the Chokecherry Blossoms shone, the herd would have shed the dead hair of winter and slicked off, ready to find the Sioux's brother, the buffalo. New colts would be racing about—then Black Wolf could smile.

He fashioned a noose on the paint's lower jaw, then bounded on the horse's back. No need for a saddle or all that.

Two other men slipped in the pen, caught their own horses, and joined him.

The Society of the Wolf was about in the snowy half light. Red Deer and Blue Fox, his brothers by blood, needed no invitation to join him. They came without his asking, regardless of his purpose, be it to hunt, fight, or to argue with the white chief at Fort Robinson for more stringy beef for his people.

"No dreams?" Red Deer asked, joining him.

"No dreams. Maybe they have stolen them too."

"Stolen what?" Blue Fox asked joining them. Obviously he had not heard their words over the scream of the wind.

"Someone has stolen his vision," Red Deer said.

"Magpies?"

"Maybe," Wolf agreed, and they smiled at one another.

If only it were the saucy camp birds who took his power. He could kill them one at a time with a small bow and arrow until all the thieves were gone. But he could never shoot all the whites; they were like the blades of grass. Those long moons he spent in Sitting Bull's lodge—listening to how they would slay so many white men and in the end—they would lose.

He could vividly recall the scalp dance after the hot dusty day's battle on the hill, when they had killed so many blue legs. Oh, how sweet the total victory! He could hear the loud chanting and the drums. Some drank whiskey. Others complained of the soldiers forted behind their packs on the hill above camp—and bragged that they would kill the rest of them too. But those that went to try soon came back and said the rest of the soldiers were too fortified up there.

Black Wolf would later learn that they were Reno and Benteen's men. It made no matter to him. Scouts came back into camp before the great dipper traveled half its way across the northern sky. They spoke of many more blue coats under Terry coming from the north. And the Cheyenne scouts said a large column with Crook on his mule leading his whole army was coming from the south.

Many of the leaders, Cheyenne, Arapahos, and Sioux, went to Sitting Bull and held a council. Black Wolf recalled the sickness he'd felt in his stomach, not for his own life but for all the women and children in camp. White soldiers had little respect for them. The assembled chiefs asked Sitting Bull what they should do. Wait and kill the arriving soldiers or flee?

"I'm going to the queen's place," Sitting Bull announced, never answering their questions. "She will keep her word with my people."

"What if she does not want you?" Black Wolf asked.

Sitting Bull shook his head. "I know I have a place up there for me and my people."

Among those assembled was Gall, who had led the most warriors the day before into the hardest fighting. Anger turned Gall's broad face black at the medicine man's words about going to Canada.

"You have not seen where we can stand on this land and fight them?" another leader asked.

"I do not wish to hide behind the skirts of some white woman like a groveling dog," Gall said, raising a cheer from the others crowded in the tepee.

Sitting Bull said no more. His dark brown eyes gazed beyond the lodge filled with angry bloodthirsty men. Black Wolf saw the firelight dance in his eyes like a looking glass.

"Are we to be become mules for whites? I am a warrior, not a plow man," Gall said, the fury still loud in his voice. "This Sweetwater land is where I choose to die. If we are strong. If our hearts are strong—"

Sitting Bull shook his head. The small thin braids danced on his thick shoulders. His actions silenced them.

"No," he began in a soft low voice. "In the end they will take this land like they took the Black Hills from us. Even without gold nuggets in the stream, they will think gold is here too, and that we are hiding it from them."

They filed outside at that. Gall raised his arm under the scarlet blanket and motioned to the distant Bighorns.

"Like the seeds of the cottonwood on a strong wind, we must drift away from this place," he said. Others still looked defiant, but the fire of their fury had already been dampened by Sitting Bull's final words.

The next morning Black Wolf took his band away. He did

not imagine the numbers of blue legs that would come to revenge the death of the Yellow Hair's soldiers. His medicine
never told him there would be so many soldiers that summer
looking for him and his band.

At last, in Moon of the Falling Leaves, Wolf brought his
people to Fort Robinson and surrendered. Once he spoke to
Red Cloud, but he did not trust this older chief. Red Cloud
had grown old and did not want to provoke the authorities.
He had lived on the dole of Army beef too long. His long
teeth had grown dull. . . .

Stung by the sharp wind's onslaught, he pushed his pony
towards Bordeaux's. Huddled on the horse's back, Black Wolf
wished for some of that summer's fierce heat. Even his fine
thick blanket did not turn away all of the cold. Wrapped in it,
he used his knees to guide the pony. The sun was only a small
white disc in the overcast sky.

They reached the trading post and put their animals in the
pen. Black Wolf carried his rifle in his arms. Red Deer and
Blue Fox joined him, adjusted their blankets, and followed
him inside single file.

When he came through the doorway, Black Wolf heard
someone coughing. A deep rasping cough like someone dying
from the lung disease. It was not the Frenchman nor his tall
willowy wife. He could see her down in the living quarters
area, busy working with her iron kettles. The tall black-
bearded Bordeaux stood behind the counter, smiling and ready
to trade.

3

"That was Black Wolf," Bordeaux said when the Sioux left. The trader took a seat in the chair beside the bed and cradled a mug of steaming coffee in his hand.

"I saw him before at the fort," Slocum managed. "He does not get along well with military." He recalled the day he'd watched the chief arguing vehemently with a Captain Brown about his band's monthly beef allowance.

"Who does?" said Bordeaux. "Those officers are like little puppets. Chest out and pompous as a Napoleon. Like they expect these proud people to come crawling on their hands and knees to their great white fathers and begging for food."

"I don't know about that." Slocum closed his eyes, and uncontrollable tears spilled down his face.

"Stay around here long enough and you will learn about their sorry ways."

"I have your bed—" A cough cut off his words. He recovered and said, "I guess I'll learn a lot."

"Don't make him speak." Jeanne narrowed her thin black arched brows at her husband. "Can't you see how sick he is?"

"I can see. He needs something to take his mind from such misery."

"Then talk about something besides the troubles of the Indians."

Bordeaux wagged his head from side to side to mock her

17

when she turned her back. "Ah, now I must cheer you," he said to Slocum.

"You may need the cheering yourself sleeping on the floor."

"Ah, oui, but you get to sleep with her."

She whirled around and glared at her husband.

"I was only cheering him up." He held his hands out in protest and both men laughed. The effort hurt Slocum.

"Oh, you are so funny," Jeanne said, and in a swirl of her skirts turned to her cooking. "Men have such funny ways." She shook her head in disapproval.

Slocum, sedated by the willow-bark tea and exhausted from his fever, fell asleep. He woke sometime in the night and discovered he indeed shared the bed with Jeanne. Her slender form was wrapped in the covers beside him; he could make out her thick braids in the orange firelight. Bordeaux was lucky to have such a beautiful and skilled woman for his wife.

Though Slocum could not imagine himself being confined to this small trading post, the company of such a woman would make the containment more palatable. Still, his soles itched more than Jim's. This vast open rolling grassland would be a cowman's paradise.

No matter how rich a livestock empire this might be, he could still hear the fiddles of the cantinas of south Texas calling him. Under the thick covers, he hugged his arms and listened to the scream of the wind at the eaves. He could feel chill on his face the chill of the wintery air that penetrated even this snug structure.

No, he belonged far south of this latitude. He lay there thinking of the shapely turn of some olive-skinned girl's hip and the warmth of the Texas sun. A shiver of cold ran up his spine. Goose flesh spread down his arms. Then with a shudder of his shoulders, he fell fast asleep again.

Black Wolf wondered about this sick man at Bordeaux's. In the dying last light of this day, he and his guards rode bent over against the increasing winds, headed for their camp. Why did the presence of one white man consume him so? Should he have learned more about him? He did not even know who he was. It would have been impolite to have demanded of

Bordeaux the man's name and business. He obviously was a friend of the trader for he was in the great sleeping place the man and his wife shared. The Frenchman must respect this one.

But what did he mean to Black Wolf? He tried to remember a face. Then the memory of a man came to him and Black Wolf felt warmer as he rode. This sick one was a cattleman. Black Wolf recalled the wide-brim hat that he'd worn last fall. The thick bat-wing chaps black on the inside of his legs from sweat. Yes, green eyes and dark brown hair. It was the Texas cowboy, all right.

A familiar feeling filled Black Wolf, triggered by a warm rush of memories. Uncertain what was happening, he felt good for the first time in a long time; then he realized that a vision was coming to him. It was strange after all his strenuous efforts had gone unanswered, but he could feel it closing in like a man about to be run down by a thousand stampeding buffalo. Why out here? He shook his head from the cover of the blanket to expose it to the night. Perhaps the sharp wind would make his senses more keen to receive it.

The others—he must send them away. His breath rushed in and out of his chest. This would be a long-awaited session for him and only he could deal with it. And he must calm down inside and approach this with reverence. At last, his hard-sought vision was coming. The notion warmed him despite the night's frozen air. His skin felt the way it did when the first soft wind from the south brought a thawing breath of spring. It was not unlike the first time as a boy when he'd sat upon a sunny hillside waiting to watch a buffalo cow in labor deliver her calf.

"Wait," Black Wolf said to the others, and slipped from his pony, holding the rein for Red Deer to take it from him.

"If you are going to pee, it may freeze off," Red Deer teased above the wind, taking the leather rein.

"No." Black Wolf shook his head. "You two must go on. I have things to do here."

"But it will soon be dark—" The man's words sounded deeply concerned.

"Go on. I will be fine."

The pair looked at each other and shook their heads in disbelief. Then, with disapproval written on their faces, they led away his buffalo horse and went off through the snow.

Under his blanket, Black Wolf felt warm for the first time in many moons. The dry snowflakes swirled around him like moths at a fire. He looked to the north. His concerned comrades, dragging his horse after them, faded into the twilight, and more snow swarmed the air about him.

He prayed to the Great Spirit for the strength he needed. Despite his prayers he began to feel his physical power drain away. *Oh, Great Spirit, help me lead my people to a way of life where the babies are fat and happy. Where no children cry at night, cold and empty-bellied. Where none will die of strange plagues and maladies. I promise you my life for this wish.*

Then he saw her emerge from the darkness and his heart stopped. Could it be she this time? Had he at last been chosen to view the Supreme One? She strode toward him in her fringed dress. Like an apparition at first, this frozen white spirit walked to him as if there was no snow to impede her steps. There was no wind. Something more like a soft summer breeze swept the long fringe of her clothing as she came closer to him.

Then he noticed the huge ivory-colored bull buffalo, only steps behind her. The animal guarded and protected her. Her dress was made of the finest elk skins. The stone-gray color was stark enough to match the colorless world. Her handsome facial features appeared chiseled by a master craftsman from ice.

"You must heal and guard this sick white man at the trading post," she said in Sioux. "He will save your band."

He marveled at the young sound of her voice. But of course she was ageless and virginal. What else could he expect? Her presence and beauty awed him too much to even ask her why he must save this white cowman. What could this cowboy do for his people? Black Wolf wanted a proud life for his people, not some beggar's existence—he felt deflated before her. This was not what he'd asked for. Hadn't she heard his needs: repeating rifles, food, robes, blankets? A new way of life to replace their imprisonment?

"Find him a woman. One from in your camp," she said.

He struggled with her wishes. Why should he—

"Not a child. He will not accept a girl." She shook her head as if to warn him.

He could see the small feathers that decorated the ermine fur in her braids. Why was she so set on him saving this white man? He hated all white men. Those pompous officers at the fort had cheated his band of their share of beef. This cattleman might have been in cahoots with them.

"Close your ears," she said. "You listen to the hollow voices of fools on the wind. This man can save your band. Is that not what you asked of me?"

He closed his eyes. She knew even what he thought. Never in his life had he known fear before. Now it grew like a fire fed pitch inside him. Not in battle had he ever experienced such feelings, even when others died beside him. Nor in the lust of a buffalo hunt turned into a stampede had he ever experienced such gut-wrenching dread. Some great hand gripped his innards and squeezed them so hard, he feared he might soil himself with urine and excrement before her.

"Did you not ask for my help?" she said, anger rising in her voice.

He nodded. Of course he'd asked for her help, but he wanted deliverance not servitude. What had Gall said at the Sweetwater camp? *I do not wish to plow.* He did not wish to plow either.

"I must go," she said. "Do you know the way?"

He nodded. He knew the way she wanted him to go. In those fleeting moments, he realized she was leaving him. Cold air sought his skin. She turned and with her shaggy companion disappeared into the falling darkness. He stood alone, shaken. The wind again screamed in his ears.

Black Wolf pulled the robe closer around him. The pits of his arms were wet. Sweat ran down his chest; it turned to icicles on his skin. He felt like a horseless man who had run for miles to escape an enemy. Exactly his feelings as a young man on his first wedding night—depleted and vulnerable. But despite being so badly shaken, he was grateful for the experience of meeting the most powerful spirit of the Sioux people.

Even Sitting Bull in all their sessions never spoke of seeing the Great One—creator of the Sioux. Had the old man ever had such an experience? Black Wolf might never know. He did know the storytellers had not come close to her beauty. But how could they? They had not seen her. He felt very small. She must have stood twice his size. Only when he was alone on the snow-swept prairie did he realize how large she and the great white one had been standing before him.

Still, her message was as bitter as the gland excretions of the skunk. It made his eyes tear as he headed for his camp. How could he be left with such a distasteful squaw's chore? He must save some white man's life. Find him a bride from his own camp. Not a child. A woman. His feet felt like great gobs of mud, growing larger and more cumbersome with each step toward his tepee.

He stumbled into his lodge on his knees and looked around. Owl Woman's face blanched and the others rushed to help him.

"You have found your vision?" Owl asked, helping to support him.

He nodded.

"And is it what you sought?"

He looked into the questioning faces of wives poised for his answer. "I must find a white man a bride from this camp."

They sat back in shocked silence.

"Tell no one." He punctuated his words with a severe frown. "I mean no one." He regretted his words. No one needed to learn of this. How could his tongue be so loose? Had he no powers left? Speaking out like a gossipy squaw. He could not believe he had spoken without any thoughts to the consequences. Things he should have held sacred flew from his lips. His mission was to lead these people, not talk on like some split-tongued raven.

"You must eat," Owl insisted.

He realized she supported him with a firm grip on his arm. They exchanged a look and her fingers released him. No. He needed no food. Better he fasted and maybe the pangs of hunger would help him to envision this bitter task. The meeting with the great spirit depleted him of all his power and strength. Only sleep would restore it. His eye lids felt lead-weighted. Perhaps his dreams would show him more about "her" wishes.

Stop listening to those hollow voices of fools in the wind. Her words scolded him again. They stung him like a flailing quirt in the hands of a powerful enemy. The stripes made cold welts on his face. Without another thought, he resolved to obey her and accept his fate.

4

"Strange thing outside," Jeanne said, looking out the window.

"What's that?" Slocum asked, busy braiding a new lead from the scraps of rawhide she'd found for him. Seated at the table, he dabbed his fingers in the raw lanolin and rubbed it with his thumbs into the leather, crossing the strands into the growing rope.

The strong stink of sheep and rawhide mingled to invade his nose, the first sign that he might be getting over the cold. It was a pungent enough odor. No doubt anyone else could smell it coming into the room.

"Black Wolf moving his camp here in the middle of winter," Jeanne said.

"That doesn't sound strange," said Slocum. He recalled the chief's wife, a tall attractive Indian named Owl Woman, who out of the blue had brought Jeanne those herbs for him. The Indian woman's sincere compassion had touched him. The medicine had not hurt him, and since he at last was feeling signs that he was recovering, he felt even more grateful. Her medicine really had worked wonders. Even Jeanne admitted it.

"No, something is going on with them," she said, standing before the window.

"You worried they'll attack?"

"No, Black Wolf and my husband understand each other.

24

They need each other. Besides, if he attacked us, the Army would punish him. Probably take him away to prison and leave his band to their own devices. He acts very protective of his people."

"I know he stood up to that captain when he considered his beef ration short," Slocum said. He looked up from his braiding when the light from the door opening and closing caught his eye.

The young Indian woman was back again. He called her "Straight Arrow." She walked with her shoulders back. Her manner accentuated her proud bustline under the deerskin dress when she swept off the trade blanket.

She had to be some rich buck's squaw, he figured. Her dress had lots of beads and her braids were wrapped in mink fur with little blue feathers. Several coins jingled in a necklace strung around her neck. She usually bought one item per visit and seldom looked around, talking softly to Jeanne. Her eyes never met his. He decided she must be married, and went back to his braiding. No doubt she would make a bedful for whoever her mate was.

"You noticed anything?" Jeanne asked, coming back to the living area when straight Arrow left the post.

"No."

"That is the only squaw who comes in here to trade since they moved their camp here."

"I hadn't been noticing."

"Slocum! You haven't missed looking at her every time she comes in."

He glanced up at Jeanne's disapproving face, then grinned at her. "So I looked at her. She's got a lot to look at."

"Hasn't been another squaw come in to buy a thing. She does all the shopping for them."

"So?" He couldn't imagine what Jeanne was driving at. So Straight Arrow did all their shopping. So what?

"Maybe she comes on purpose to see you."

"Aw, I doubt that. What have I got? You don't reckon she thinks I have an unending supply of beef, do you?" He dabbed more lanolin on his fingertips and continued braiding the rawhide.

"Men don't need to have more than good looks for some women."

"She's probably married." He wanted to think of a dozen reasons why Straight Arrow was coming in the store. The other women were too bashful to risk entering the post. She spoke a handful of good English. He'd heard her speak to Jeanne. The others didn't speak any English. He had to stop braiding and undo his work—he had miscrossed a plait. What other reason could he think of for her being the only shopper?

"I don't think she's married," Jeanne added with a wink.

"I think she is." He went back to plying his leather. Jeanne didn't know everything. His sore nose was crusting up inside. Maybe the worst was over. He would have to pay more attention to this shopper.

"Next time she comes in, let me wait on her," he said.

"Your funeral." She grinned, then poured fresh coffee in his tin cup.

"Be sure to put on a nice one. You mean, after her husband kills me for flirting with his wife?"

They both laughed, and Bordeaux came in the front door.

"Funny, am I?" he asked, shedding his buffalo coat and putting up his cap.

"No, we are talking about Slocum's admirer," she said.

"Who's that?" he asked.

"The tall Indian girl that comes in here all the time."

"Her name is Blue Water," Jim said, and took a seat at the table across from Slocum.

"And what's her husband's name?" Slocum asked, watching Jeanne close for her reaction to the answer.

"She isn't married."

"Not married? Why, she must be twenty." Slocum could hardly comprehend the notion that she wasn't wed. Such a pretty girl that age and not married? Sioux women found husbands soon after puberty. By tribal standards, she was practically an old maid.

"Why do you ask?" Jim said.

"You didn't notice that she does all the shopping in here for the other squaws?" Jeanne shook her head in disbelief at her husband.

"I noticed she had some Grand Tetons." He stuck out his chest, then ducked her slap at him and shared a big smile with Slocum.

Both men hushed at the sound of men and horses outside. Bordeaux rose to his feet. Three scruffy-looking men in buffalo coats stormed in the trading post door.

"Set up the whiskey," a one-eyed man said, and Slocum didn't miss the way he looked at Jeanne either. As if she were some kind merchandise for sale. Bordeaux rose to his full six feet and went to wait on them.

"Sorry, gentlemen. I can sell you some, but we don't serve whiskey inside the post."

"We can pay for it." The one-eyed man paused to stare at Slocum for longer than what would be considered friendly. At last he turned back to Bordeaux. "Then we'll take it outside and drink it. Damn unhospitable to me, mister."

"Sorry you feel that way," Bordeaux said, and produced two bottles.

Slocum noted the younger one was a breed. Hardly more than a kid. The other was a thin, older white man with a poor excuse for a white beard and mustache. His facial hair looked scraggly. Slocum wiped his slick fingertips on a rag and considered the .30-caliber Colt in his right boot. These men were unrepentent hardcases and might try anything.

"Name's One-Eyed Jacks. You ever heard of me?" The man dug in his coat pocket and produced some silver coins to pay Jim. With a slap, he put them on the bar.

"Jim Bordeaux. My wife, Jeanne, and Mr. Slocum."

"Slocum, huh? You ever been to Y City?"

"Time or two." Though Slocum thought long and hard, nothing on this Jacks came to mind.

"Seen you there a couple years ago."

"I must of been driving cattle up there then," Slocum said.

"You were, for a man name of Cruthers."

"I made a few drives for him."

"Yeah, let's go, boys. This man says we can't drink it in here. Pardon, ma'am. Boscoe and Injun here, they ain't go no manners." Jacks doffed his shapeless brown-felt hat to Jeanne.

She nodded and pursed her lips.

"You sure got enough blanket-ass Injuns around here," Jacks said, and then herded his cohorts out the door.

Bordeaux and Slocum shared a hard look. Those three spelled trouble.

"I am going up and tell Black Wolf about them. They might cause him problems," Jim said, putting on his buffalo coat.

"Be careful," Jeanne said, and hurried across the room to help him into his jacket.

"I'll watch things," Slocum promised him.

The threesome wasn't half as bad right now as they might be liquored up. Slocum dabbed his fingers in the yellow lubricant. The smell of raw sheep again went up his nose, and he resumed his braiding. He tried to recall the time in Y City. But all he could think about was bailing three of his young cowboys out of the local jail for raising too much hell. They'd delivered a herd of cows to a rancher north of there. An uneventful drive, as he recalled. If he'd met Jacks before, it would come back to him. The three were no more than frontier trash by his standards, the kind of cutthroats that preyed upon isolated immigrants. Rapes and murders by their kind went unprosecuted all over the prairie. Atrocities to both white or red were not uncommon. They would do to watch.

"You know them?" Jeanne asked, sounding concerned.

"I don't recall Jacks. But I've met a million men in my life."

"You would never forget him either. That blind eye needed a patch." Beneath the blue dress, her shoulders gave an involuntary shudder.

"I suspect the other one needs to be permanently closed too."

She nodded as if to escape her own thoughts of the men.

Bordeaux came inside stomping his boots and hung up the coat. "Black Wolf says he will tell his people to stay away from them and maybe those hardcases will ride on in the morning."

"Perhaps we need to keep an eye on them," Slocum suggested.

"Might not be a bad idea. They're camped on the creek."

"Good, we can take turns."

"You don't need to be out in that cold," Jeanne said with a look of concern.

"I'll have to start getting my strength back sometime," Slocum said.

Jim rose to Slocum's defense. "I think he's doing very good."

"He doesn't need a relapse." She drew a deep breath and sighed as if outnumbered.

"Jim may want his bed back." Slocum winked at him.

She made a face and busied herself sewing on a quilt.

"I want you well too," Jim began. "I want for you to take these furs I have all baled to Independence for me, and pick up the supplies I have ordered from Chouteau's."

"That ought to be a warm trip." Slocum chuckled at the notion of freezing himself to death hauling furs overland for Bordeaux.

"There's usually a break in February when you can make many miles. But you must get there and started back before the ice breaks or you have to swim the rivers."

Slocum nodded. This was not Bordeaux's first request for him to make that drive. So far he had shrugged off the man's efforts. Soon he would have to decide whether to take the job or not—he dreaded it, but still felt obligated to the man. But when spring grass looked close he planned to take his pony and ride south. Before he ever stayed up this far north again in wintertime, he wanted some Apache to stake him out on an anthill. He'd spend all next summer in south Texas getting warm to the bone.

They took turns checking on Jacks and his bunch. Jim went first and Slocum slept the first two hours. Then Jim shook him and set the rifle down by the table.

"No problem, they're pretty quiet. They turn in, you come back and wake me up, I'll give you my side of the bed back."

Slocum laughed. In Jim's big buffalo coat, he tugged on his gloves, pulled on the wool Scotch cap, and tucked his ears under the flaps. With the heavy Winchester .44/40 in his arms, he eased out the front door of the trading post into the crisp snowy world. In the starlight he paused to check the chamber by easing down the lever. At the sight of the brass cartridge, he shoved the lever back and clicked the hammer on safety. His boot soles crunched on the snow, but he knew the sound was louder to him than anyone else.

He squatted on the bank to cut his silhouette and studied their dying fire. Two men were seated before it. He could hear their words. Not all were audible, but the whiskey had loosened their tongues and he could hear the profanity.

At the slight rustle of something, Slocum whirled and saw three armed Sioux squatted on their heels in the dim starlight. He nodded and turned back. Obviously the Indians were also leery of the three and taking no chances.

One Indian joined him. He recognized the chief when he eased down beside him. The aroma of sage campfire smoke clung to the man.

"You can go to bed." The Sioux tossed his head in the direction of Jacks's camp and then, with a head shake, dismissed the hardcases as nothing to worry about.

Slocum shook his head. "No. Bordeaux and his woman need more time alone."

Black Wolf indicated that he understood. "Come to a lodge. I have tobacco."

Slocum followed the man. The other two Indians acknowledged him in passing. Damn strange for a wild Sioux to do such a thing as this for a white man. Slocum knew plenty about them from his days scouting for the Army. Lots of tame Sioux got along well with the whites, but the wild ones had no use for his race. They could ignore a white man to his face. Maybe they thought he was part of Bordeaux's business and they needed to get along with him.

Slocum bent over to enter the tepee, and in the glow of the fire he saw her. Straight Arrow, whom Bordeaux called Blue Water, sat across the circle of rocks and faced him. The orange light danced on her handsome face.

He removed his cap and ran his fingers through his too long hair.

"Sit," Black Wolf said, and motioned to the ground.

Slocum smiled at his words. Obviously this man was used to giving orders; his impatience was obvious. Had he invited

Slocum here for a smoke or more? Slocum wondered what the woman's role was in this meeting.

Black Wolf put his rifle outside, then came back and opened the scarlet blanket. Slocum could see the bone decorations sewn on the chief's blouse. Black Wolf picked up a pipe and packed it with tobacco from a small pouch, so intent on his job that Slocum had to watch him. Then Blue Water raised up, leaned over the small hot fire, and held a flaming stick for Black Wolf to draw on.

The pipe began to send up smoke, and she sat back. Her eyes avoided Slocum. He rubbed his whisker-bristled mouth and wondered what would happen next. Jim and Jeanne had better be taking good advantage of his absence. Maybe Black Wolf and Jim had planned it this way. Amused, Slocum nodded as soberly as he could when Black Wolf handed him the stone pipe. He drew in and found the tobacco aromatic enough. Better than some Indian smokes he had taken before— those had cut out the lining of his mouth and throat.

To be polite he suppressed a need to cough. Black Wolf puffed some more and then handed the pipe back to him. Whatever this ceremony was, Slocum wondered what part the women played in it.

"The spirits have spoken to me," Black Wolf said, and after he took another pull, set the pipe down. The sweet smoke from the bowl carried to Slocum's nose.

He nodded and waited for the man's words. Many times before he'd sat in lodges seeking peace or help from some red man like Black Wolf. They were usually orators and savored the role.

"This woman, Blue Water, is like a sister to me. Like my own daughter. She has been chosen by many brave men in my tribe. They have brought many horses to her family's lodge and asked for her, but she refused them. When her parents died, as chief I accepted her father's role. They came to me. Brave men with horses and riches. But she would not have them. She told me once she saw a face in the river."

"A face?" Slocum frowned at the man, then looked hard at the unmoving woman across the circle.

"*Your* face," Black Wolf said.

"I am the wind." Slocum shook his head. "I can't stay here. She does not understand. I'm . . ." How could he tell them he was a hunted man? His face was on wanted posters. Two brothers out of Fort Scott, Kansas, were searching the West for him. He couldn't stay there any more than he could anywhere else.

"I could not marry her," he said when neither Black Wolf nor the girl answered him.

"If you had a wish like she has and you only held it for a short while, wouldn't that be better than never having a dream?" Black Wolf asked.

"It would not be fair to her."

"To her? She wants the dream."

Slocum pressed his hands on top of his crossed legs and drew in the deep smell of the sage fire. The chief was serious about this. Blue Water had come in the store under any excuse to see the man she'd seen in her vision. But Lord, why him?

"Stay with her tonight. If she is not a good one to stay with, go back to the trading post." Wolf's dark hand cut the air as if to slice them apart.

"But I must—"

"Look at her. Is she ugly? She is old enough for a white man?"

"Old enough?" Slocum asked in dismay

"Most white men don't want young wives."

"Wives?"

"She is Blue Water. She wants to be your woman."

Slocum blew his nose, stuck the rag away, then looked hard at him. "I need to go check on those men."

"No. My brothers will make sure they will disturb no one. Tonight stay here." He pointed to the ground.

Black Wolf rose and said something guttural in Sioux to her. She nodded eagerly. Then he turned back to Slocum. "Stay here tonight."

And Black Wolf was gone.

Somewhere far away a real wolf howled at the star-pricked sky. His deep yodel carried across the frozen land, and Slocum studied the flames in the fire. He undid the greatcoat and shrugged it off. Blue Water started to rise, but he shook his head to stop her. He could do it himself.

Then, with the burden of it gone, he flexed his shoulders and removed the cap. He looked across at her expectant face and tossed the cap on his coat. A million questions crossed his mind. This woman—what did she expect? How much did she know about a man and a woman? Indians lived very openly. She had to know.

He looked hard at her and tried to decide how to start. Without a word, she rose like a limber willow until she stood over him. Her arms went above her head; she began to remove the beaded blouse. He swallowed as the curtain of deerskin lifted, exposing rounded breasts that shook as she stripped off the top.

He dried his palms on his pants. The emptiness in his gut grew more intense. Forced to swallow, he watched her untie the strings at her waist. The garment slipped off her long hips and soon she stepped from it. The shadow of the center line traced over her flat stomach into the dark V of her pubic area. Then her long fingers extended to him and invited him to join her.

He rose on shaky legs, mesmerized by this siren. They stood in the red-orange light of the tepee and she undid his shirt. He looked into the dark pools of her brown eyes. When she stripped the shirt back and exposed his underwear, he took her in his arms. She dodged his mouth, but he sought her.

His hands slid up and down her sleek skin from her hard butt to her shoulders. At last he tasted her mouth and the honey slipped from her lips as she began to understand his purpose. Their actions soon consumed them.

He toed off his boots. Their fingers madly fumbled at the job of stripping him of his clothes. Pants, then his one-piece underwear, until he could not resist and moved in to hug her ripe body to his own. A cool draft swept over his skin. Unfettered, he savored her body with his kneading hands and mouth.

She pulled him down onto her blankets. Her eyes glazed over; he could hardly believe his good fortune. He spread her long shapely legs and moved between them. He nosed his hard probe into her moist gates and she stiffened, held her breath. Then he started to ease himself inside the doorway. She threw her head back and gave a sharp cry as he parted her maidenhead. She clutched him so desperately, he feared for her discomfort. But twice she went limp in pleasure, and each time he smiled down at her groggy look. Then slowly he reawakened her spirit to a frenzy, then came to the place where he sought the deepest part of her.

He clutched both sides of her hard butt in both hands and drove his shaft home. Fireworks ran through his vision. His entire backside felt emptied and his strength exploded away. He rolled off and gently fondled her breasts.

"Blue Water," he said, and closed his eyes. Oh, hell, what would he do next?

5

Wolf squatted in the snow. No sounds came from the camp of the bad white eyes. Good, they would have no trouble with them. Still, Bordeaux had told him well—to be aware. He looked up and saw through the tepee's skin the outline of the girl stand and take off her blouse. He smiled to himself. Then Slocum's silhouette shown on the translucent tepee side as he rose to his feet. Who could resist a virgin served on a board to you? He looked like a man to him. Then Wolf saw the two of them hug each other.

He glanced off. What else must he do next for this man? He waited a long time and at last he heard her cry out and recalled another time he heard such a sound from a woman. It was the night that he took Owl Woman's virginity. Good, he hoped the mighty one had learned of what he had done for the white man this night. How would one man, an outsider, ever save his band?

He rose wearily and went back to his own tepee.

The sound of breathing was even. Children, wives were all asleep. For a moment before he went to his place of sleep, he squatted down to warm before the fire. He felt the blanket being removed from his shoulders.

Owl Woman looked into his face, curious to know how his plan had gone. He drove his middle finger inside his other fist and then smiled at her. She nodded her approval and motioned for him to join her. Good. They did not make love often these days. With everyone asleep, he could savor her body as he used to when they were young and free people, when the two other wives and responsibilities as chieftain did not interrupt their lives. He felt himself growing hard in anticipation of their union.

What else must he do for the White Buffalo Woman and this white man? He wanted to giggle while laying down on top of her. He was a boy again—a horse stealer, who took many from the Crows. A buffalo hunter—oh, he was proud of it all back then; how his dusky pink erection stayed so hard for so long a time; how his beautiful wife would run like a wild deer. And like a great stag, he would chase her and give her enough of his shaft to exhaust her spirit into submission. Then he would release her to chase her again. This night they would quietly savor each other's bodies, the intimate closeness of sharing, and then sleep.

Slocum awoke in the morning to find the gray light of predawn had already crossed the plains. It was later than he'd wished to rise. He stood up quietly and dressed. Now he had to explain everything to the trader and his wife. The night before he'd left the trading post to guard them all, and then had found Blue Water. He glanced down at Blue Water's handsome sleeping face. Wild horses could not keep him away. He would be back.

Halfway across the yard, he spied the hardcases' shaggy horses at the hitch rail. Jacks was back inside the post. No telling what he was up to. Slocum stopped, bent down, and drew the small .30-caliber Colt from his boot. He slipped the revolver in his side pocket and hurried on his way.

Jeanne's scream cut the early morning air. Slocum started down the bank and faced the barrel of the skinny one's Sharps rifle.

"Get them hands up in the sky, mister!" the man ordered.

Nothing to do but obey. He dropped the Winchester in the snow and raised his hands. Then under the man's directions, he moved to the wall of the dugout. He tried to see what was going on inside, but from the corner of his eye he couldn't see much.

The kid came out and hung a sack of whiskey bottles over the saddlehorn of one horse. He gave Slocum a mild look and went back inside. The skinny one shook the muzzle at him to keep Slocum in place.

"Don't try nothing, I got me an itchy finger."

"Your neck itching?" Slocum asked him.

The man blinked and shook his head.

"It will when they stretch it."

"You talk big for a man liable to die with his boots on."

Slocum shook his head in dismissal. "If I was you I'd be whipping that horse to death and getting the hell out of this country 'cause when the word gets back to Chouteau's you robbed one of their outposts—your life won't be worth a skunk hide."

"This ain't one of their's." The man made a sour face of disbelief.

"Guess you'll learn that when you wake up and some big Osage has got a skinning knife stuck to your throat. You'll know who owned it."

"Shut up," he said as the kid came out with his arms full again. "I ain't talking to you. Tell that damn Jacks to get out here," he said to the kid.

"What the hell's wrong with you?" Jacks shouted from inside.

"This Slocum says this is a Chouteau outpost."

"So?" Sticking his head out the doorway, Jacks looked up and down at Slocum. "Tie the sum-bitch up."

"Them Choteaus got mean henchmen."

"Tie him up and let me worry about the fucking Choo-toes. Kid, get the rest of that stuff."

Slocum didn't know what condition the Bordeauxs were in. If they had hurt her . . . He wanted Skinny to turn away for a moment. Then the man looked aside to see about the kid and let his guard down.

"Look careful," Slocum said. His fist held the small pistol from his pocket. Skinny's eye bugged out. He dropped the Sharps like a wooden figure. Then something shattered Slocum's head and he felt himself pitch forward into the snow.

•   •   •

He awoke with his sore skull in Blue Water's lap. The pounding in his temples was loud and pointed. He made out Black Wolf squatted before him and two other Sioux. Jim paced the floor beyond them.

"Jeanne—" Slocum half-raised, and then he saw her, coming with a steaming pan of water and a white towel. She was all right. Thank God. He settled back and smiled up at Blue Water. She nodded, looking relieved that he was coming around.

"We want to go after them," Black Wolf said.

"I told him the agency would have a fit," Jim began. "If you miss the roll call, they will mark you as a renegade. That gives the military the right to gun you down."

"He's right," Slocum said, exchanging a nod with Jeanne as she put the hot towel on his head. Obviously they wanted him to tell them what to do next. Jim, of course, had to stay there with her.

"You have a nasty knot in back of your head where he hit you," she said with a look of disapproval.

"He did it right."

"We can overtake them," Black Wolf said, still on the matter of Jacks and his gang.

"I better go try and do that," Slocum said. "No sense in making the military angry."

"I will go with you," Black Wolf said.

"When is the head count taken?" Slocum asked Jim.

"Saturday," Jim said.

"Today's Tuesday?"

"Wednesday."

"I lost one. I wasn't out that long?"

"Nope."

"Saddle some horses. That bunch gets on that whiskey, we may catch up with them in a few hours."

Black Wolf's men rose and went to saddle horses for them. Slocum sat up and looked into the eyes of Blue Water. He turned to Black Wolf.

"Tell her I will be back when we get these men."

"She understand English good," Black Wolf scoffed. He rose and swiped the dirt from his backside. "Tell her yourself."

"Be careful," she whispered in his ear.

He nodded and stood, despite Jeanne's protest. On his feet, he blinked, then reached back and rubbed the tender goose egg on the back of his head. Jacks had sure put one on him. Lucky that was all that had happened to him. He sure owed those boys for that knot back there. The headache pounded at his temples. He offered Blue Water his hand and pulled her to her feet.

"Jeanne, look after Blue Water until I get back."

She nodded and then smiled smugly. "I told you so."

Jim handed him the small pistol, which he slipped in his coat pocket. He hefted the .44/40 and considered what he must do next. Blue Water gave him his hat. It hurt to wear it, so he pocketed it. The sun was up and made some heat outside. It was still cold, but the solar heat helped some.

Jim returned with a sack of provisions for them to take. Black Wolf's men delivered the horses. The trader ducked inside and came out with sack of corn for horse feed. Slocum hugged Blue Water. They shared a private look; words were not necessary. They both felt the strong bond. He turned and shoved the repeater in the boot, then mounted his pony. He had enough regrets about leaving his newfound woman to make his guts roil. Black Wolf was already in his saddle. They left the post in a stir of dry snow. The tracks went east.

Wolf did the tracking and they trotted their mounts. The sun rose, and by midday they had reached another dugout. Cautiously they studied the pens and the surroundings to be sure it was not a trap.

A body sprawled in the snow before the door. Black Wolf nodded grimly at Slocum.

"A Sioux will be blamed for this," Black Wolf said, and booted his horse off the slope.

Slocum acknowledged the man's words. He rose in the stirrups and searched around a last time for any sign of the outlaws. Then he followed the chief's horse down the steep grade.

"This one is dead," Black Wolf said, squatting beside the form.

Slocum turned him over and saw the nasty black bullet hole in his forehead.

"Don't move, you savage bastards, you." They looked up in time to see a woman wearing a white shift fill the doorway, holding an ancient shotgun pointed at them.

"Wait!" Slocum said.

Too late. The scattergun belched shot and gun smoke out the muzzle at both of them. The blast went into snow between them. Slocum could see Black Wolf was unhurt, and he scrambled for the shotgun. The woman's face blanched; then her knees buckled and she pitched forward.

Black Wolf sprang past her and looked inside the doorway. Slocum caught her, took the Greener away from her, and eased her onto the ground.

"Nothing in here," Black Wolf said.

Slocum knelt down and rolled her over. "Get some blankets for her."

Her face was that of a girl. Perhaps eighteen. He frowned at the bloodstains below her stomach on her shift. What had those bastards done to her? Raped her, probably took turns. She needed medical attention. Take her to Fort Robinson was all he knew to do.

Black Wolf helped him wrap her as she began to come out of her faint. Her blue eyes opened and blinked, then flew wide in fear. Her hands shot protectively to her crotch and she started to protest.

"Lady, we ain't them. They're gone," Slocum said to ease her concern.

She still screamed for them not to do it to her again. Nothing Slocum said helped. At last he carried her screaming and kicking inside the dugout, and put her on the bed. She immediately huddled in a fetal position and went to sobbing, her whole body shaking under the brown blankets.

Black Wolf squatted and stared out the doorway. "Spirits speak to her."

"And those bastards must have raped her," Slocum agreed. He dug in his pocket and found two small cigars. He'd forgotten them. In all his sickness the thought of smoking had never occurred to him. It looked like a good time to have a smoke and figure out their next plan.

"How far away are they?" Slocum asked.

"They took some fresh horses from here," Black Wolf said, accepting the cigar. "Means they can go further."

Slocum struck a match and held it out in his cupped hand for Black Wolf to light his cigar. Then the match grew too short; he struck another lucifer and studied the scarlet-soaked snow bathed by the setting sun. The day was over. They had a new problem. The woman needed medical attention. The chase was over. They also needed to do something with the dead man's body.

Slocum watched the glow of his cigar, listening to the woman sob on the bed. The smoke filled his lungs and relaxed some of the muscles in his saddle-sore body. He'd been laid up for too long with his illness. He exhaled and the smoke spread away from him.

He looked over and wondered what Black Wolf had on his mind. Obviously the man hated to give up the chase. Slocum felt tired to the bone and closed his eyes. Jacks would pay for this crime, sooner or later. So would his men.

The woman sat up on her knees. Tears streamed down her red face and she screamed. "Don't do that to me again!"

Slocum closed his arms around her in an effort to comfort her. "They're gone, girl. They're gone."

6

Slocum dug a shallow grave inside the animal shed for the man's body. He turned up chunks of frozen ground under the straw and manure until he finally got below the frost line. Then he shoveled out a hole deep enough to lay the body in, and placed boards over him before he refilled the hole so the wolves couldn't dig him up.

"Her brother," he said to Black Wolf, who held the light for him.

Black Wolf agreed. He had heard the crazy white woman say it was her brother, not her man. Black Wolf was concerned. He could tell she was not right in the mind. It was not good to mess with such people. They could bring bad luck. He would be glad when this man delivered her to the fort as he spoke of doing. It served the Army right to have her; maybe it would bring them bad luck too. But he must watch and be certain nothing happened to Slocum—and that this crazy woman did not hurt or cast a spell on him.

Never in his life as a warrior had he been given such a difficult task. First, he'd talked to Blue Water and explained this man was something important to their spirits. She should take him and protect him with her life if necessary, for her people needed his medicine. The girl had understood. That was a miracle.

After her first night with Slocum she'd come all upset to

42

his tepee. With tears in her eyes she'd told Owl Woman that she did not know why he'd left her. They had not argued. She had given him her body and would do his wishes. Where had he gone?

Then word had come that those evil white men had robbed the trading post, and Black Wolf had rushed to the dugout. The robbers had tied Bordeaux and his wife, and Slocum lay on the ground. Blue Water had quickly cradled his head.

Black Wolf had breathed much easier when the big man spoke at last. For a while he'd wondered if he had lost the one who would save his people. Now, while they buried this dead man in this cow-smelling place, the bad white men were getting away, and he feared they would never pay for the attack on the post.

"That's good enough," Slocum said, and tossed the short shovel aside. The dirt was mounded over the grave. He looked satisfied, and motioned to Black Wolf he was ready to leave.

Black Wolf agreed. Slocum had labored much for this dead man's spirit. This boy would go to the good land. Wherever white men went. His body was intact. Then Black Wolf wondered if white men would be there too in his next world. He wouldn't want to go if they were. He hoped only Indians were allowed in, and even some were not welcome. He didn't want to spend his days listening to some Pawnee brag about his victories—that would be worse than having a loose-tongued wife.

He carried the lamp and walked beside Slocum. What would this man do next for the crazy woman? Better they left her and went on. No, he knew Slocum had his mind set on taking her back to the authorities.

Slocum took the light from him and blew it out at the front door. He paused to turn his ear to the cries of the wolves. They were chasing something out on the prairie. Not much game left for them with all the buffalo being slaughtered for their hides. The wolves had even attacked people, and of course livestock, to satisfy their voracious appetite.

"She's calmed down," Slocum said under his breath when they entered the room. The girl sat in a rocker wrapped in a blanket, her red face dry of tears.

"Why did you bring that blanket-ass Injun in here for, Jed?" she asked Slocum. Then she pumped the wooden rocker back and forth like child in a swing.

"He's my friend Black Wolf. He has no tepee. He only needs to stay here tonight, then he will go back to his own people."

"You know I don't like dogs or Injuns in my house."

"Just for tonight, Pearlie."

"Maybe one night, but I think he's got bugs, Jed."

"No, Black Wolf has no bugs, Pearlie."

"All them Injuns got them."

"He's different." Slocum built the fire up and set an iron skillet on the sheet-metal stove's top.

"What you messing with, Jed?"

"Going to fix us some food, Pearlie. We need to eat." He shook his head at the Indian, who squatted on the other side of the stove; Slocum could handle her alone.

"Don't be wasting my good bacon on no gawdamn Injun now, Jed."

"I won't," he said, busy slicing off white ribbons of it from the large chunk of smoked meat.

"That's got to last us till spring, remember?"

"I know, Pearlie. You just rest."

With bacon sizzling in the grease, he sliced a pan of potatoes into cubes. Seated on the edge of a straight-back chair, he absorbed himself in the task of cutting them up. How Black Wolf sat on his haunches so long without getting stiff was beyond him. Indians must be cut of different timber.

The spuds soon sizzled in another skillet, and Slocum sat back. The grave digging had left his back tight and the aroma of food cooking made his mouth water. Some outfit. A crazy woman in a runaway rocker, a Sioux chief who hadn't said ten words in a day, and Slocum—the cook for the camp.

But it was better Black Wolf said nothing. That way he didn't remind the girl that he was still in her dugout. She and her brother must have spent a while building this dugout. They had a good larder of food. Potatoes and turnips were all stored in the cellar beside the house. A big crock of sauerkraut was made up, but Slocum had never liked it.

The woman could not stay out there by herself in her condition. She might have been touched in the head even when her brother was still alive.

And Jacks and his no-goods hadn't helped her. The fact that they'd gotten away upset Slocum. But their trails would cross again and this time Slocum would be ready.

The following day, in late afternoon, they rode into Fort Robinson. A wind swept the powdered snow across the recently scraped walkway. A thin veil of white blanketed the surface. Slocum kicked his leg over the saddlehorn, hopped down, and reached up to help the girl down.

He set her on her feet and said softly, "We're here, Pearlie."

She blinked her eyes at the two-story brick barracks. "Some school house, Jed?"

He agreed, and took her personal things wrapped in the blanket Black Wolf had carried over his lap on the ride there.

"Mr. Slocum," Captain Brown said, coming out the front door.

"Captain Brown. This is Pearlie and she was attacked. Her brother, her only living kin, was killed. She needs some care."

"Results of an Indian raid, I take it?" The man looked at the girl as if outraged by the notion. She ignored him and acted busy examining the architecture of the headquarters as if the captain wasn't even there.

"No, they were white men. The same gang that robbed Bordeaux's trading post."

"I see. Take her to Lieutenant Grimes. He can find quarters for her."

"Captain, here are her personal things. I have buried her brother and been in her company long enough. She is now a ward of the U.S. Army." He thrust the bound blanket into the shocked officer's arms.

"But—" the red-faced Brown sputtered after him.

Mounted, Slocum saluted the wide-eyed Brown, who in turn thrust the blanket into some guard's arms and ordered him to escort her inside. Then he turned to frown at Slocum. Before Slocum reined his horse around, he gave Brown another salute off the brim of his wool cap. He could also swear that the corners of Black Wolf's mouth were turned into a grin.

7

Jim Bordeaux hid any disappointment at the news that they didn't get the robbers or the loot back. He stalked the dugout floor while Slocum sat at their table. Blue Water stood proudly behind him. Black Wolf squatted on the floor, and Jeanne rushed about refilling their coffee cups.

"What they got was only a small amount of cash and some trade supplies like lead and a small keg of gunpowder," Jim said, "I had the rest hidden. I have offered a reward for their capture. I sent word to Chouteau's today. Someone will collect the reward."

"If we hadn't stumbled onto Pearlie—" Slocum gave a shrug. There was nothing they could have done but brought the poor girl Fort Robinson.

"Now that you are well, do you feel ready to take my furs to Independence?" Jim asked.

It was an outright question. Jim expected an answer from him. The man desperately needed someone to take his furs in for him and come back with trade goods for the spring season. Slocum slumped down in the chair and considered the entire matter. What if the Abbott brothers showed up in the middle of it and he had to leave? That pair of bounty hunters from Fort Scott that dogged him for years. Who would take over the train?

"How much help have you found?" Slocum asked, hoping

46

maybe the trip would be impossible without any workers.

"I have talked to the Portugee. He will go."

Slocum shook his head. "Two men alone can't take that many pack animals to Independence."

"I will go with you," Black Wolf said.

Slocum blinked at the chief, and Jim whirled around to stare at him too.

"Blue Water and Owl Woman can do the cooking," Black Wolf continued.

"That would take a permit," Bordeaux said with a frown.

Black Wolf held up three fingers. That meant he and the other two leaders of the camp would go along.

Slocum considered the matter. A Portugee US man he did not know and three Indians and two women. That would be some pack train to cross that snowy wasteland between there and Independence. There would be blizzards, and drifts as high as a man's head. They could face any kind of weather out there. It looked like an impossible task to him.

"There you go," Jim said, a smile of relief on his face.

"It ain't likely that Brown or that strait-laced Colonel Wilton is going to give all those Sioux passes to leave the reservation."

"You have a point, Slocum." Jim suddenly had a look of grave concern.

"How else will we learn the white man's way?" Black Wolf asked.

"He has a better point." Jim grinned. Slocum felt trapped. This all sounded so easy in the warmth of that great room— to set out on a six- to seven-hundred-mile trek. Using Indians who were warriors, not workers, while Slocum and those squaws did all the work.

"I will go to the fort at first light and request the passes for Black Wolf, Red Deer, and Blue Fox," Jim offered.

"Hold everything," Slocum said, still not convinced. "I haven't agreed to this. Who is this Portugee?"

"Oh, John?" Jeanne said, with her prettiest smile. "He is a very hard worker. He'll do the work of three men."

"How hard is he to get along with?" Slocum asked. There

had to be something wrong with the lone white man they could find in all of western Nebraska.

Jim shook his head. "Portugee John is a good man. I swear he is."

"We could use a few more hands," Slocum said, still uncertain. "And what are we going to do for animal feed? Horses can't paw snow and pack furs all day."

"We can spare enough corn to get you well across Nebraska. Then you can buy more from the farmers along the way."

"That's going to take extra horses to pack that corn."

"Plenty horses," Black Wolf said, and sliced the air with his flat hand.

Plenty horses maybe. In Slocum's book those runty Indian horses couldn't carry much either. But despite his protests, Slocum considered himself outnumbered. Then he felt Blue Water's hand on his shoulder to reassure him it would work. She had seen his frustrations. For a woman he had only known for one night, she warmed him with her concern.

"You will do it?" Jim asked him pointedly.

A moment of silence. Slocum nodded in defeat and everyone cheered.

"I have a buffalo hump roasted for this occasion," Jeanne announced.

Slocum exchanged a look with Blue Water. In the flickering lamplight, she stood very tall over him. Jim went for a bottle of wine to celebrate.

When the meeting and feast were at last over, Slocum and Blue Water hurried to her tepee. She fed the fire to drive the deep chill from the interior. He sat and watched her working. The small flames reflected off her smooth copper skin, and her long subtle fingers fed the fire until the larger sticks burst into tongues of red.

"Have you ever seen the white man's world?" he asked her.

She shook her head. "Is it pretty?"

"No—but it is busy," he said, wondering how else to describe it to her.

"Busy?"

"Yes, lots goes on there."

"Is it like a great Indian camp?"

"No, bigger than that. More buildings like the fort, only many more buildings."

"Are there many buffalos?"

"No, they have cows to milk."

"To milk?"

"You will see it all." He grew tired of explaining and waved her over. She came and knelt before him. With her head bowed, the great braids rode on top of the blouse that molded her breasts. He swept her into his arms. Tomorrow, yes, tomorrow, he could tell her more about the ways of white man. Her voluptuous body in his arms, he stared into the dark pools of brown—lots of woman to hold. This time her mouth did not avoid his kiss.

"I won't issue permits to those savages even to go to Hell under any circumstances!" Captain Brown pounded his desk top with his fist. "If it was the last thing I did in this damn Army! I won't—"

Slocum watched the cords in the officer's neck draw tight. His face flushed with rage and the tiny red wormlike blood vessels in his nose surged to the surface. Despite Bordeaux's diplomatic approach to the man, getting passes for the three Sioux sounded impossible to Slocum. They'd have to try something else.

"Those three were at the Little Big Horn. Did you know that?" Brown asked, swinging his arm around as if pointing to where the battle had occurred. "Why, they probably killed Custer themselves."

"I didn't come to argue that." Jim's voice grew louder. "There are no men to hire to take my furs to market. These Indians are willing to work. It is a matter of commerce. They are on the reservation now."

"No!"

"Then, Jim, I guess we will go to see this man's superior," Slocum said.

"Colonel Wilton won't sign it either."

"First, we must ask him," Slocum said.

"He won't." Brown sat back in his chair and looked smug.

"I am sorry, but you will just have to find workers for your train elsewhere."

In the hallway, Bordeaux made a face at Slocum. "He is a madman. They want them to be civilized. Yet they won't let them do anything."

"I agree there ain't much forgiveness in his heart for Indians," Slocum said, glancing back to be certain his comments were unheard.

"Have you met the colonel?"

Slocum shook his head.

The enlisted man at the desk looked up. "May I help you?"

"We need to speak to Colonel Wilton on a matter of business."

"Your names?"

"Bordeaux and Slocum."

"I will tell him you are here."

Slocum listened to a woman's voice beyond the open door berating someone. "I can't stand that woman," the voice said. "She is obsessed and needs confinement. I understand she has relatives in eastern Nebraska. She should be sent there at once."

"My dear, the poor girl has been through an ordeal," said a man's voice.

"An ordeal? I should say so. John, you must send her away. The sooner the better."

With that said, the matronly woman came storming out of the office. Her bustle twitched like a fat goose as she hurried down the hallway without a civil word to either Slocum or Jim.

"Gentlemen, what may I do for you?" Wilton asked them from the doorway. A tall man in his blue uniform, he filled the space.

"We came to see about taking a pack train of goods east," Jim began.

Slocum saw a flicker of light in the man's blue eyes.

"Let me get this straight," Wilton said after the trader explained their needs. "You want passes for three Sioux males to help make the trip? We don't even count the squaws, but we don't let them know that, of course."

"Exactly."

"You were the one brought that poor girl in, weren't you?" Wilton looked at Slocum.

"Yes, we found her."

"Good. I'll give you those three passes for Black Wolf and the others, and on your way you take Pearlie back to her relatives."

"Wait," Slocum said. "This isn't a wagon train. We're taking furs on packhorses. No one will have time to take care of her. Look after her."

"You brought her in, didn't you?" Jim said. "You're taking two Indian women along with you. They can tend to her needs, can't they?"

"Yes, but—" Slocum could see this whole episode becoming more complicated by the minute.

"Gentlemen, you need three passes," the colonel said. "I need that poor disturbed woman taken to her relatives. I think we have reached an agreement." Wilton looked hard at Bordeaux, who nodded, leaving no option for Slocum but to agree.

Thirty minutes later, they were leaving the building when, with his coffee cup in hand, Captain Brown intercepted them.

"You may have won this round. I understand Wilton issued you those permits. But if those heathen bastards cause one moment's trouble out there, it will be your responsibility."

"Captain Brown, thanks for your warm encouragement. Now let us by," Slocum said with little time for the man.

"I can close that trading post of yours down any time I like, Bordeaux, and don't you forget it!"

Slocum turned back and glared at the man. "You threatening my friend here?"

"And I can turn down any herd of cattle you bring in here."

"I'd say you had a bad case of too-tight pants, Captain," Slocum said, then nodded to Jim that he was ready to leave. He'd had all of the cocky little man that he wanted. If they hadn't needed those passes so badly, he'd have shown Brown a thing or two. *Vindictive bastard.* It was officers like him who made it so hard for the Indians to ever find a normal life.

Mounted up in the midday sun that glared off the white landscape, they trotted their horses back to the post. Slocum knew the weather was only a brief respite from the severe blasts that he expected to return any day. The temperature must have climbed to twenty degrees. In places the wagon tracks they rode over showed signs of melting under the sun's power.

He considered the trip with dread. Instead of agreeing to take the train, he should have used these days to hurry south. A shiver of cold shook his shoulders beneath his clothes and coat despite the warmth of the rays on the canvas. He belonged in Texas. Even daydreaming about the subtle-bodied Blue Water, while he rode back, he still did not belong in this ice-locked land.

"Wolf ever speak to you about me?" Slocum asked as they drew their horses down to a walk letting them breathe.

Jim shook his head. "No why?"

"Something there I am not sure about. He has a keen interest in my safety. I first thought it was his chief ways, but I can't put my finger on it. For some reason he is very damn protective of me, since that first night I went to check on them hiders."

"He must like you." Jim shrugged.

"Maybe—" Slocum had no answer. Some time he would out and out ask the man. And Blue Water was his gift. He knew that from the first night. He doubted she had ever seen his image in the river. What about this trip back east made it so important to the chief? He shook his head and dismissed his concern. They still had miles to ride.

At the post, he put the horses up. In minutes, Blue Water came running to find him, fringe flagging her way from her tepee. She quickly began to help him brush down and care for the two animals.

"This is the work of women," she said, out of breath, and took the brush from him.

"In my world, we share some jobs."

"Share?" She blinked.

"I am not afraid to do women's work, as you call it."

She nodded. "Did the Army give you the passes?"

"Yes, they did. But we must take the white woman that Black Wolf and I found with us."

"The crazy woman?"

"Yes."

She brushed down the horse's side with the brush, and Slocum glanced over to see her response.

"They are afraid of her?"

"I guess. Are you?"

"No, but I will be very careful around her. The spirits possess her mind."

"Something sure does," he said, and used his jackknife to clean the packed snow from the horse's frog. Then he dropped the foot and straightened.

"We will celebrate tonight," she said, and grinned at him. "I soon must go help Owl Woman get the food ready."

"Go do that. This is all that I am going to do to the horses."

Slocum gave her shoulder a hug, kissed her cool cheek, and then watched her hurry off. Blue Water never walked. He admired her enthusiasm.

He hurried on to the trading post. He could use some of Jeanne's good strong coffee.

"The Indians are going to celebrate this business," he said, looking through the small six-pane window.

"Yes. Black Wolf left excited," Jim said. "I hope you aren't too angry with me."

"What?" Slocum turned and blinked at the man.

"I mean, I sort of imposed on you to take this job."

"I owed you."

"You owed my wife, not me."

"I owed you because you let her nurse me back to health."

"I don't let her do anything," Jim said under his breath.

They both laughed, and Jeanne looked back at them mildly from the fireplace. Good thing she did not hear them.

"More coffee?" she called out.

"No, I better get back to my tepee."

She smiled at him. "You may become our longtime neighbor."

"Maybe."

He left his canvas coat unbuttoned and hurried into the bright sun from the dugout to the cone-shaped tepees. As he drew closer he noticed three or four woman working on something. Blue stood up holding an object and the other women seated on the ground were busy working. Within twenty steps, he could see Blue held a fat black camp dog by the heels and was bleeding it. The sharp odor of viscera stung his nose. Owl was finishing skinning another one. She ripped the hide from the pinkish carcass. The two other women seated on the ground were busy butchering the dressed dogs and tossing the pieces of meat in a pile before them.

A large knot formed behind his tongue; he forced down the urge to gag. He had forgotten; that's what Sioux considered a delicacy. Dog.

8

Across the sparkling white ground, Black Wolf could see them coming from many directions in long lines. Most all of the Sioux nation assigned to the Red Cloud Agency would be at Bordeaux's by dark. It would be a good thing: powerful magic from so many other medicine men to send them on this long journey. They came on foot, in wagons, and on horseback. By evening, there were over two hundred Indians, men, women, and children, about the camp. Black Wolf knew word traveled fast when a celebration was planned. One band hauled half a freshly killed buffalo to cook and serve at the festivities. A member of Bone Beater's group had killed it near the Black Hills. But that village was willing to share their great meat with their brothers.

Black Wolf knew all these people who came, and he spoke in pleasantries to the various men when they arrived. Tepees went up and someone brought in a wagon load of sawed logs to burn. It was Big Stick, who owned the cross-cut saw that his wives used to make the uniform-sized chunks of firewood.

Maybe Black Wolf should consider finding such an iron beaver for himself on this trip. Big Stick had made much money from his business. The officers at the fort paid him well to bring them a wagon load of wood. He was richer than Buffalo Hair, who sent his women out to pick up dried buffalo chips by the wagon load and later sold them. Or some others who collected the bleached bones of the buffalo and like low-life grave robbers cashed them in with one of the white traders further north.

Red Deer was close on Black Wolf's heels. When they started back for their camp, he spoke.

"The white man Slocum does not like dog meat."

"He tell you?" Black Wolf asked.

"No. His woman spoke about it to your women and I heard them talking."

"So?" What difference could that make? White men ate things called kraut, which he hated. The notion of the bitter taste of the stuff in the barrel that Slocum had found made him shudder. Even Slocum had agreed it tasted bad.

"How could he take a Sioux wife and not like dog?" Red Deer asked.

"The man is an omen." Black Wolf shook his head. "Even I have no idea what his purpose is, but he is important, or the White Buffalo Woman would not have told me so."

"The woman Blue Water must like his bed."

Black Wolf agreed with a nod. He knew nothing more of the man except that he was very kind to her. Some men did not have to beat their women to show they were big men. Others could learn from his ways. He also gave her pots to cook in, while the Sioux let their wives trade for them if they had goods to barter with. These things he knew about this man.

He also used his mouth on hers. It was a secret language between them. Slocum would kiss her on the face, and Blue Water's eyes would light up and she would give him a lustful look. Perhaps it kept the heat of passion inside her hot, the way stoking the coals with a stick every once in a while made the rest catch on fire.

White men had their ways. He was anxious to learn more. They must have powerful balls too. They produced so many more offspring than Indians. Black Wolf recalled as a boy in the south, how he'd watched the never-ending line of wagons passing each spring going west to fill the land beyond the sunset.

He'd always hoped they would keep going and fall off the

earth. But they must not have, at least not enough. They still came. He shook his head in fury. Why couldn't he go back and live in his father's time when white men made no difference? When the Sioux ate buffalo all the time, when their women made great stores of pemmican from the sweet chokecherries, fat, and dried meat.

The time when the disease was unknown that had scarred and killed so many. Smallpox, the white man called it. Big Pox, he called it. Whole villages died from it, some people so scarred they never looked another in the eye. They wore their scars like sinners. He pulled the blanket over his shoulders and went to find his ward.

How could he explain to the others who came to the feast that this white man had his protection? He must do it quickly before some buck that Blue Water had declined to marry took offense at her giving her virginity to a white man. They did not need to know the White Buffalo Woman had told him so. He would only share that with his own society members, and maybe Sitting Bull when he returned from Canada.

Before Slocum's tepee, he squatted and waited. Those inside would soon discover his presence. He did not wish to disturb their privacy. Soon Blue Water came out, saw him, and ducked back inside.

"Black Wolf is outside for you," he heard her say in English.

Then Slocum emerged in a new buckskin shirt with a blanket over his arm. He nodded to Black Wolf and Red Deer.

"I don't know much about such festivities," he said, and squatted with the two men.

"You have big appetite?" Red Deer asked.

Slocum nodded. "I don't wish to offend your friends," he said.

Black Wolf nodded. "You are one of us. I will introduce you as a brother."

"Not all Sioux will like that," Slocum said.

"All birds do not fly away together either," Black Wolf said, a little amazed by how well the man understood his people. "You are my guest."

Slocum nodded. Then he rose and flung the blanket over

his shoulders. The three of them stood and went to the main area where flames licked at the logs Big Stick had provided.

Black Wolf did not wish to miss the opportunity to learn what Slocum knew about such things. He took him aside by the sleeve and showed him the wagon and the crosscut in the bed. The red lights of the fire shone on the recently filed teeth.

"Can you show me how to make them chew like a thousand beavers?" Black Wolf asked.

"Yes, I can show you how to use that," Slocum said. "But you must show me how to feather an arrow."

"Feather an arrow?" He frowned at Slocum, then quickly agreed. There must be something in feathering an arrow that Slocum needed. Black Wolf seldom did it anymore; using the white man's powder and ball was easier and quicker. Many days he'd spent selecting arrow shafts, filing down steel tips with hard rocks, and using the feathers of the hawk to send them straight for the heart.

Why did this tall white man want such training? How did Slocum know about fixing the teeth on Big Stick's crosscut? Perhaps white men were born with such knowledge. That was it. He led Slocum to where the men had gathered sitting on the buffalo robes around the fire.

He sat with Red Deer behind him and Slocum on his right hand to show his respect to his special guest. Blue Fox joined them and nodded to the other men.

"There are plenty of Sioux here," he said, and sat on Black Wolf's left.

Then came the old man Yellow Elk, withered and bent with the infirmities of his age. He stopped, and Black Wolf beckoned him to take a place. The old man nodded and sat down at Black Wolf's knee.

"This man is your brother?" Yellow Elk asked in Sioux, indicating Slocum. His paper-thin skin was drawn tight to his cheekbones and rheumy eyes were tucked deep in the sockets lined with crow's feet.

"Yes," Black Wolf agreed.

"He must have done much for you."

"I cannot say."

"Then you have spoken to the spirit one?"

"Yes, I spoke to her."

"I once spoke to her. Many years ago. Had I known I would live so long, I would have asked her why."

Black Wolf laughed at the old man's words. He elbowed Slocum and translated. "Yellow Elk wants to ask the Great Spirit why he is still alive."

Slocum answered him with a polite nod and grin.

"What did she tell you when you spoke to her?" Black Wolf asked the frail man in Sioux.

"That someday when my dick would not get hard, there would be more widows in my camp than the men could handle." Yellow Elk nodded gravely and said softly, "That day has come."

Black Wolf nodded soberly; he had heard the old man's words. With much effort, the wisp of a man rose to his feet, spoke politely in Sioux to Slocum, as if he could understand him, and moved on.

"How old is he?" Red Deer asked.

"Old." Black Wolf shook his head. He had no idea how many winters Yellow Elk represented. His own manhood still worked, and he dreaded the notion it might someday quit becoming hard enough to penetrate a woman. But while as a boy he could do so many things, today he could do only some of them. Perhaps the power went away like that, and one day it would no longer matter.

Maybe to become a white man was not the worst of his worries ahead. But if he had to become white and then he couldn't bed a woman, that would be far worse than he could have ever imagined. He gave the blanket a hunch with his shoulders, enough to settle it on his neck. Then he strained in his crotch until he felt the entire length of his dick curled in his breechcloth. It was still there and still worked.

He studied the flames licking upward, the heat on his face and chest. Deep in the orange, yellow, and blue tongues of fire he searched for a vision. A sign to tell him what he must do next. But the inferno only consumed more logs without a vision for him. Sparks flew up in an explosion when Big Stick's wife tossed more wood on it. But there was nothing for him to see.

9

Slocum watched them shuffle and stomp in the firelight. "Hey-oh, hey-oh," chanting voices resounded in the night. Blue Water brought him some roasted buffalo. He felt grateful that she respected his request and did not serve him any dog.

The beat of the drums sounded like thunder on the wings of an approaching summer storm. Tortoise-shell rattles joined the music. Shrill eagle-wing-bone flutes pierced the night air. Despite the cold, many of the dancers shed their blankets and stomped in buckskin clothing. Disregarding the chill, several danced only in their breechcloths.

Slocum felt moved by their actions. It was more like a religious experience for these people than a dance—they were there to pray for the success of his expedition. It was similar to a war party starting out on a mission against their enemies or a horse-stealing expedition. This was a preparation ceremony for the warriors' souls.

Despite the shortage of food, one band had generously donated half of the only buffalo killed since fall. When it was eaten, that might be all the meat they would have until the next month's beef allowance. Slocum knew any longhorns the agency allotted them would be thin and tough. Left to fend for themselves, the southern cattle would have quickly lost their summer fat in such cold and bitter weather.

"What bush gives the white man flour?" Black Wolf asked, then wiped his lips on his sleeve.

"A grass," Slocum said.

Black Wolf nodded and looked at the meat left on the great rib, already full but unwilling to quit eating. "I want to see such grass."

"There will be acres of it in the spring."

"You must plant it like corn?"

"Yes."

"Why do all the things white men use to eat have to be such work?"

"There are too many white men for the wild things to be enough to feed them."

"The Sioux have lived for many years on the plains and fed off the great buffalo herds. Now their brown brothers grow fewer. Once you would wait three days for their passing in herds so wide you could not see across them."

"Yes." How could Slocum explain to this man that at the current rate of buffalo slaughter, he too would have to grow wheat and raise cows or live off the government dole for the rest of his life?

Two large beaded moccasins stopped before him. Slocum raised his gaze to look up at the man. A big hulking Indian stood with his bare arms folded, a mask of contempt written on his face. His words in Sioux sounded like a challenge.

In a flash, Black Wolf was on his feet and shouting at the man. His guttural words were sharp and his directions for the man to leave easily translated. For a long moment, even the chanting stilled. Everyone stood poised in place. The two men glared at each other, only inches apart. Anger flared in both men's eyes.

Then the larger man nodded, said something softer, and moved away without looking again at Slocum. Black Wolf dropped back to his place. Red Deer spoke from behind them and Black Wolf nodded in agreement. The stomping resumed and each dancer acted as if nothing had happened.

"That was Horse Man," Black Wolf said, his gaze intent on the dancers and the fire beyond. "Once he came and asked for Blue Water."

"And she refused him?"

Black Wolf nodded. "He is a large man, but his thinking is slow. I think he is over his anger. But ashes can smolder and the fire recover."

"I will watch for him."

"Good." Black Wolf grinned and nodded in approval.

"Black Wolf?" Slocum waited until the Sioux acknowledged him. "I have fought my own wars for years. I appreciate your looking out for me, but I can take care of myself."

"You are my guest. It is impolite to insult a guest in my camp."

"Fine. In the morning, you plan to send boys after the horses so we can pick out the pack animals?"

"They will return before the sun is there." He indicated the noon zenith.

"Good. Tomorrow morning, I will go see about the Portugee and his carts."

"His horses are powerful."

"Draft horses," Slocum said, recalling Jim's description. The words must not have struck a chord with Black Wolf. He merely agreed. There were two large horses, one each for the carts, and the rest of the bales of furs would be loaded on ponies. How much could they stand to carry in their weakened winter condition? Two fur bales per animal? Not much more if they had to be able to flounder through the snow.

Slocum dreaded the first few days. The Indian horses would be wild. They would be lucky to make many miles. Then there would be the problems of harsher weather moving in and stopping them. He pulled the blanket up and hunched his shoulders beneath it. Despite the reflected heat of the fire, a wave of cold ran up his spine.

Blue Water came and squatted beside him. "You look tired. Maybe you should go to sleep."

"I do not wish to insult Black Wolf," he said to her.

Then he felt the chief's hand on his sleeve, and a wide knowing grin spread over Black Wolf's face.

"It is time for you to go to your lodge."

Slocum shared a grateful nod with the man. Then he nodded to Red Deer and Blue Fox and rose, feeling stiff from the long hours of sitting. The dancing could go on for hours.

Blue Water led the way with her long fingers in his grasp. They slipped through the crowd and crossed the starlit packed snow toward the conical outline of her tepee. Somewhere a wolf raised his plaintive voice to the night and carried above the sound of the dancers behind them.

They reached the entrance. She ducked and went inside. Slocum looked around carefully. His breath caused clouds of vapor. Nothing moved; even the camp dogs, full of scraps, were resting. The wail of the music carried to him, now more distant. Satisfied nothing was wrong about their camp that he could detect, he bent over and entered the tepee.

"You are worried?" she asked, kneeling at the fire ring and feeding it back to life.

"I am thinking about the long journey. It will be hard on you and Owl Woman."

"I am a Sioux woman."

"Yeah," he agreed, amused. "You are that. But the travel will be hard. The wind will fight us. Storms—" He shook his head and then swept off his cap.

"Tonight we have this lodge," she said.

"Yes, we better enjoy it."

"Come." She stood, quickly shucked her long skirt, then peeled off the leather leggings. Firelight danced on her shapely legs. He rose to his feet, moved to her, and took her in his arms, filled with a great need for her body. His palm ran up her flat, muscled belly and soon clutched her breast, feeling the rock-hard nipple poking his palm.

His mouth sought hers and he tasted the honey of it. Their tongues clashed like swords and the heat of their needs fired his brain. Her frantic fingers undid his waistband, shoved the pants off his butt, and pulled him to her. His mild erection slipped between her satin legs.

She raised her left knee and he nosed himself into her slick nest. With her knee pressed to his side, he began to hunch in and out of her well. She grasped his neck with both hands to hang on and murmured in pleasure. His fingers were filled with the firm flesh of her butt. He savored each stroke in her passageway. On and on he went, savoring the waves of her contractions and the thrill of his penetration.

At last, she motioned toward the pallet and he agreed. They briefly separated, and his throbbing sword ached for the captivity of her sheath. On her back, she held out her arms, knees drawn up and spread apart for his entry. They resumed their madness.

Like a barrage of thunderstorms, they reached heights that made her swoon, and then they began again. Her hard bare heels kicked him in the butt, and the muscles of her stomach drew up tight under his own corded ones. Pelvic bone to pelvic bone, they ground out the last vestiges of pleasure from each other. Then, when the head of his dick swelled to twice its normal size, she cried out, "Yes."

He exploded inside her.

Soon after, they fell apart into each other's arms as her breathing slipped into a whisper. Yet he lay awake and considered many things. The saddles, the packs. Tying on the loads. While the women were experienced, they seldom made such lengthy journeys. Thus, when they did raise a gall on a horse's back, it could heal before they moved on again, or another horse would be used to replace the first.

But in this case, they must make the animals do for the whole trip there and back. Strange too that he had not so far met this man they called Portugee John. What was he like? Slocum would learn in the morning. He stared at the poles crisscrossed at the top of the tepee where the flap released the smoke. How long had these people understood the draft of their fires? Who had taught them the certain ways the poles were to be crossed to withstand wind and brutal storms? Yet each time they went to a new place the women reset them, and they were almost a fortress against nature's blasts.

He could hear the dancers' song and music in the distance, and wondered if they would go on all night. Since he was an outsider, it was hard to understand their intense feelings for such activity. This evening he had seen their pride return. The same long-faced individuals that had arrived earlier by horse or rickety wagon now showed an intensity, a fervor, that returned them to the time when the buffalo passed by in herds too large to count. They were living the past again.

Then he heard footsteps on the hard snow. Then sharp voices in the night, followed by the sound of a thud. He reached into his pants and grasped the Colt from his holster on the fly. He stuck his head outside, and saw the outline of two men dragging another away by his arms.

The cold sought Slocum's face. He drew a sharp breath.

"It is all right," Black Wolf said, squatted to the side of the opening.

"Did he—"

"He has learned a lesson."

Slocum realized who it was. "I can handle him."

"No." Black Wolf rose slowly to his feet. "He will not get another warning."

Slocum uncocked the Colt. He watched Black Wolf walk away after the others, then went back inside. In deep concentration, he lay back down.

"You are all right?" Blue Water asked, snuggling against him.

"Yes."

"Good," she mumbled, and went back to sleep.

But sleep avoided Slocum. His eyes grew weary, but the lids refused to close. So he lay with her in his arms, a firm breast buried in his chest and an arm flung over him. He waited for dawn.

10

On the rise in sight of the cabin, Slocum reined up his horse beside Jim's. The trader indicated this was Portuguee John's place. Planted before them stood a low-walled log structure and a great tepee. The skin sides were decorated with drawings of horses and riders in a great buffalo hunt. A menagerie of yellow and gray-black dogs ran out to bark at them. The man's squaw came to the front door, garbed in a snowy elk-skin dress that hugged her wide girth and ample breasts. The garment was covered in colorful bead work, obviously a sign of their wealth.

When they drew up at the hitch rack, Jim spoke to her in Sioux and she nodded, then motioned for them to come inside. A half-dozen small children with dark eyes peeked at them from behind her skirt, then fled at the two men's approach from the hitch rack.

"This is Raven's Wing," Jim said, introducing her to him in passing.

"Howdy, gents," a dark-complected man said, holding up a crock jug. "The drinks are on me today. Anyone crazy enough to go off and try to take a caravan to Independence this time of year needs his head examined or more whiskey."

"Portuegee John, this is Slocum."

The man switched hands with the crock. He looked swarthy enough, and his facial features were small and hand-chiseled.

But his language was not what Slocum expected from a Portuguese. He exchanged firm grips with a leathery callused palm.

"My God, man, you must be crazy too." Then Portugee John laughed and sloshed whiskey in the tin cups on the counter.

"Must be," Slocum agreed, and looked around the cabin. The walls were decorated with bear skins. Light came in through a row of clear glass bottles that were lined up in a frame to form the two windows. Snowshoes, skis, coats, winter apparel, and other gear hung on pegs. The neatness of the room's construction attested to the man's skill at making things. In the corner, bales of fur were stacked.

"Portugee also trades with the Sioux," Jim said.

"Yeah, but not like Bordeaux. He is the master." The man raised his cup in a toast.

"He says you have some draft horses to pull your two carts," Slocum said as he clinked cups with them.

"Big horses. They are in good shape."

Slocum nodded in approval. The whiskey went down smooth enough to warm his ears. It amazed him some that the man had no more accent than *he* had. Obviously there was a yet untold story about this squat man who acted more like a town merchant than a frontier outcast.

"I'll be there at Jim's when this late-rising sun finally peeks over the horizon," Portugee John said.

"Who will drive the second wagon?" Slocum asked.

"Ah, my oldest son, Beaver Tail. He is twelve and ready to become a man. You will meet him when he finishes chopping wood for his mother."

Slocum nodded. Portugee John was a pleasant surprise. It eased Slocum's concern to know that someone would be able to continue if he had to leave the train for any reason.

Later in the afternoon, he and Jim rode back toward Bordeaux's place after eating a meal of elk with potatoes that Portugee John had grown in his garden that past summer. His stomach full, the wind gentle for a change, Slocum felt sleepy in the saddle under the sun's warmth riding back to the dugout.

"He is educated?" Slocum asked.

"Yes, I think he is."

"What is he doing out here?"

Jim shrugged. "I never asked. Plenty of people out here are running away. From a bad marriage, debts, a criminal act, maybe life itself, no?"

"I understand. I expected to meet a man who spoke broken English." Slocum chuckled to himself. "Maybe wore a patch over one eye and wrapped his head in a bandanna."

"Ah, no, Portugee John, he is more civilized than that."

"They must sleep in the tepee. I saw no beds in the house."

"I think you are right. I never noticed before. He must make that concession to her, no?"

"I guess so. I hope those shaggy Indian ponies of Black Wolf's make it." Slocum thought about the herd driven in the day before by the youths. They were winter-raw and slapsided, more mane and tail than horse. After seeing the disappointment on his face at the sight of them, Blue Water had assured him they were tough. They would need to be.

"Will you join Portugee John and me when this trip is completed?" Jim asked, booting his mount to keep up.

"No. I can't. There are men that ride my backtrail. That's why I almost told you I couldn't do this. But I see with Portugee John along, if I am forced to leave, he could handle it."

"Yes, I consider him a good man. But these men who ride your trail, as you say?" Jim frowned at him in question.

"It happened a long time ago. A man's son was killed and I was blamed for something I never did. The witnesses are dead or gone now and this man is rich and owns the law. He pays the bloodhounds that track me."

"Who are these men?"

"The Abbott brothers from Fort Scott, Kansas."

"I will be aware of them, my friend."

"Thanks. I guess the colonel is sending Pearlie out in the morning?"

"Ah, yes. I am sorry about that."

"Pearlie isn't any more problem than this snow and cold will be."

"I hope it stays this mild the whole way there for you."

"It won't," Slocum said ruefully, and kicked his own horse into a trot. He had things still to do.

At the trading post, he and Blue Water went over the various packsaddles and pads. They had enough equipment; much of it Black Wolf had borrowed from other bands. No doubt some was stolen from the Army, perhaps even booty from the battle at Little Big Horn. It made no difference. They loaded food, grain, and some hay from Jim's stack that the Portuguese could carry in his wagons. Then the fur bales were packed on the ponies. While Slocum had seemingly unlimited horses to pick from, the notion of packing and unpacking so many each day would make the job insurmountable for his few hands.

His next problem was Black Wolf. The man had to do more than squat on his haunches in the snow and watch the women work. How could Slocum impress the chief and his lieutenants that they needed to pitch in if they were ever going to get there?

"Do Sioux men ever pack horses?" he asked.

Blue Water frowned at him.

"I need to tell the men they must help pack horses each day or we will never get there."

"Tell them," she said with a shrug as if that was no problem.

"Where did you learn all your English?"

"From a missionary woman who came and lived with the Sioux many years ago. I can write my name. I could read, but I have not done that in years. I use to—Jesus loves me, this I know," she began to sing. "For the Bible tells me so. Little things to him belong. We are weak but he is strong."

"You didn't forget much she taught you." He smiled at her.

Blue Water grinned back with pride. "I loved those days. My people had plenty of buffalo. Our camp was always full of Sioux songs. No one sings anymore. This woman, Mary Stuart was her name, came among us. She had many powers and some were afraid of her. They would not let their children go near her, but my mother said, 'Go to her and learn her powers.' So I did."

"Why did you not take a husband?"

"I had a vision when my blood first flowed. The White

Buffalo Woman spoke to me and said you were coming."

"Then did she tell you that I was here?" He looked hard at her for an answer.

For a long moment, as if uncertain, she chewed on her lower lip. "I was told you were here."

He decided that was enough. No need to upset her. Besides, how did you mix Christianity and Sioux religion into one? Obviously it had complicated her life.

"In the morning we go," he said.

"I am ready," she told him, resetting the blanket on her shoulders and moving to his side. "We should go to the tepee perhaps?"

He looked down and listened to the slap of the leather fringe on her skirt and blouse. One more night alone in her lodge—after that they wouldn't have the opportunity to make love so freely in their bedrolls with the others close by.

Good idea. Slocum checked around. Everything looked in order. There was not much more he could do. He only wished the foreboding feeling about the trip that rode deep in his gut would go away.

Black Wolf watched the two of them head for the tepee. He knew what they would do next. The past few days, Black Wolf had spent much time with his youngest wife. Her wish to bear a child for him had plagued him. Perhaps he was growing too old and his seeds were dead. Maybe now she would get with child. Greater than her being with child would be for their offspring to live. It was so much sorrow to lose a newborn, and he had lost many. Each one's death felt like an arrow in his chest. Babies that never cried, babies born too soon to live outside their mother's womb.

Maybe he should take the younger woman along on this trip instead of Owl Woman. Then each night he could replant her. But the notion did not appeal to him. She lacked the strength of Owl Woman to work. Besides, in the blankets, she reminded him much of a white man's cow in heat. She simply lay there as if obligated.

Some young men were envious of a man like him who had three wives. He could recall in his youth thinking that if he had three wives, he would use one before he arose in the morning, one at midday, and the other twice before he slept. But in those days, he always was hard. In those days, one romp on top of a woman called for another right away. Now his need grew less, much less.

The only woman that he really enjoyed in his blankets was Owl Woman. She was the one who made it exciting even after so many winters together. If he did it for pleasure, he did it with his first wife. The other two were an obligation, though he tried to hide that fact from them and not show any favoritism. There was enough jealousy in his lodges already.

Three wives were as trying as caring for a white man. He had wondered about the man's journey with Bordeaux to Portugee John's place. It was a relief to him when Slocum returned unharmed.

Who could have bothered his ward? Maybe the foolish one who hated that Blue Water did not marry him and took up with Slocum. He would bear to watch until they were gone on their way. Red Deer had followed the man on the night of the dance, and struck him over the head when he approached Slocum's lodge.

Black Wolf looked up and noticed a troop of soldiers coming. Their blue overcoats sparkled against the white world. Captain Brown rode in front and they had two Indian police riding with them. Traitors to his people. They wore the blue uniform because they'd never earned the respect of their own people and become chiefs. Instead they'd joined the white man so they could order their own brothers and sisters around.

He recognized the police too. One was short and fat. His name was Fast Deer. The other, a tall one, was Whistling Elk. Whistling Elk saw him and rode over. Black Wolf could see the crazy white woman was with them too. She rode with a sidesaddle.

"The captain says for you to line up all the men in camp for a roll call," Whistling Elk said in Sioux.

"This is not the time. Some are not here." Black Wolf bristled at the demand. Did they expect his people to stay in their tepees and wait for a call from the blue legs? The food they supplied was only enough to starve on.

"Where are they?" The policeman's face turned black with anger.

"Some are hunting. Others are gathering wood."

"The captain said for all the men in camp to answer the roll call."

"He should let us know. This is not the new moon."

Whistling Elk looked undecided. At long last he reined his government horse around and rode back to where straight-backed Brown sat his horse with the troopers.

"He won't like that answer," Fast Deer said, leaning forward on his Army saddle.

"I am not his dog."

"Captain Brown thinks you will go on a big raid while you are with this train."

"He is crazy."

The policeman shrugged under his thick blue woolen coat.

Whistling Elk came back. "He wants all the men back in camp before you leave here. To be counted."

"There are some many miles away cutting wood." Black Wolf could hardly believe the man's demands. He watched Bordeaux in his buffalo robe stride across the frozen snow. Maybe he could talk some sense to these people.

"What is it, Black Wolf?" Bordeaux asked when he drew closer.

"They want a head count. No one is here. They are cutting wood and hunting."

"Why do they want that?" The big man frowned and put his hands on his hips.

"Captain Brown, I guess." Black Wolf shrugged.

"I'll handle him."

Black Wolf watched the big man stalk off across the powdery snow toward the soldiers. Bordeaux was mad. The anger was written on his face. Black Wolf wanted to laugh, but he contained himself. He closed his blanket with his fist to shut out the draft of the cold north wind. Perhaps the captain had been a member of Custer's army and had been with Benteen and Reno on the hill.

He listened to their angry voices on the wind. His own distrust of Brown ran deep. Since they'd come in to the agency, Black Wolf had watched the red-faced officer glare and point at him many times. He could never hear the man's words, but he knew they were words of hatred.

Bordeaux came stalking back, still flush-faced.

"He says he has his orders and can't do anything else."

"I can send boys after the others, but many will be days getting here."

Bordeaux looked off in the distance, obviously troubled at Black Wolf's reply. Then he shook his head warily.

"We must tell Slocum," Black Wolf said. Perhaps the tall white man knew a way. After all, the Great Spirit had said he would save Black Wolf's people.

"Where is he?" Bordeaux looked around.

"He is in his lodge with his woman."

"Helluva time to go bother someone, but he needs to know."

Black Wolf agreed and they hurried across the packed snow for the tepee. Black Wolf wanted to look back, but he wouldn't give the captain the satisfaction that he had disturbed him. Perhaps Slocum could undo this. He hoped so. They would soon run out of hay for such a band of horses if they were forced to stay there much longer.

Black Wolf knew Slocum, like Bordeaux, would be angry. At the tepee, Black Wolf stole a glance back when it was obvious Brown wasn't looking after them. He drew a deep breath to settle himself. And Sitting Bull thought the queen's redcoats were difficult! He'd better not come home.

11

Slocum quickly pulled on his pants. "I'm coming," he called.

It proved hard for him to dress with Blue Water stealing kisses from him. He should know better than to teach an Indian woman to kiss. Most of them got so they really liked it. Finally she settled back on her legs and with a look of reluctance, allowed him to dress.

Her long pendulous breasts shook with an appealing firmness when she pulled a blanket up to cover herself. Slocum rose and finished pulling on his pants. He gestured toward the entrance.

"Invite them in," he said.

She nodded and rose, holding the blanket closed. At the flap she stuck her head out and spoke to them.

He finished tucking in his shirt and motioned for the two men to take a seat. Both of them sat down, but from the troubled looks on their faces, he knew something was wrong.

"Brown is out there with that woman," Jim said, taking a seat on the robe-strewn floor. "He ain't letting anyone go till he takes the roll."

"Why?"

"He claims that Black Wolf and his men just want to get off the reservation and that others are waiting out there and they'll join up and have a war party."

"He's gone mad," Slocum said, combing his hair back with

his fingers, from the corner of his eye watching Blue Water dressing behind the men's backs. "There's no way to do a roll call."

"He says that no one's leaving until he has his way."

"Why didn't he say something at the fort?"

"You've got to remember, he was not going to issue those passes."

"Yes." Slocum dropped his gaze and considered the small fire in the circle. "So he extracts his revenge for going over his head with this."

"He is a very vengeful man, no?"

"You say he has the woman with him?"

"Yes, why?"

"Did he bring any gear to camp, like a wagon?"

"No."

"Then he's going back to the fort tonight to sleep. That means he will have to leave shortly to return there by dark."

"Perhaps they have bedrolls on their horses. I never checked."

Bordeaux looked at Black Wolf, who shrugged. He didn't know. Slocum went over several things in his mind. Brown had Pearlie. The women at the fort did not want Pearlie back there. The poor gal was the reason they'd gotten those passes in the first place. It was time to dicker with Brown.

"You've got a plan?" Bordeaux asked.

"I think a good one. Let's go see Captain Brown."

Several of the soldiers had bought firewood from some of the squaws and were building fires. Others stomped around to keep their feet warm. Brown remained with his sergeant and the flapping guidon for the company.

Slocum noticed the Indian police were off to the side talking to a squaw. With Bordeaux and Black Wolf, he crossed the hard crusted snow to where Brown stalked back and forth.

"Captain Brown, sir," Slocum began.

"If you have come to argue about my orders, save your words, Slocum." The man raised his whiskered chin in a defiant pose.

"I am certain that the colonel will be pleased when you return with Pearlie to the fort tonight," Slocum countered.

"What?" Brown blinked his dark brown eyes in wonderment. "She's your ward now."

"No, sir. Those tribesmen of Black Wolf's are miles from here. It will require many days for them and their families to return. You must take Pearlie back to Fort Robinson for now."

"Just a damn minute. That crazy—" He glanced over to where Pearlie stood chattering with three enlisted men, then turned back. "I am leaving her here."

Slocum shook his head. "No, you won't. Until I leave here with that pack train, she's your ward, Captain."

"I was ordered to—"

"Fine, you mount up and return to the fort. In the morning we will send some young boys on horseback and they will take the word to the others. When all the band is assembled, you can bring her back."

"Gawdamn you, Slocum!" Brown's face reddened with anger.

"Captain, if you intend to inconvenience me, I see no reason to please you."

"Damn you, you haven't heard the last of this."

"Oh, I think so. Black Wolf, Red Deer, and Blue Fox are leaving with me for Independence at first light. I can take Miss Pearlie along or you can keep her."

"The colonel isn't going to like being blackmailed."

"No, but he don't want Pearlie back either."

"Sergeant, get that woman over here." Brown scowled at the three of them.

"Yes, sir," the sergeant said.

The war had ended. Or maybe only a battle. Brown would be gunning for Slocum from here on out the way he was gunning for Black Wolf.

The sergeant brought Pearlie over to them. Brown removed an envelope from his pocket and handed it to Slocum.

"All the information on her kinfolks is in there."

"You haven't seen my calf today?" Pearlie asked them, looking blank-faced. "She wandered off and I hope the wolves haven't eaten her. She's golden brown and white."

"Not today, but we will look for her," Slocum said, and

touched his hat brim to Brown. It was a cheap victory. There would be more battles.

"I really am concerned about Bessie," Pearlie said.

"I can imagine you are. Come along, Pearlie. Blue Water has some hot tea for you." Slocum guided her by the arm toward the tepee.

"Those soldiers are going to look for Bessie too. They were nice men, those soldiers."

"Yes, they were," Slocum said, hearing the noncom give the orders to mount up.

"How you ever did that I don't know," Jim said under his breath, with Black Wolf on his heels, hurrying to catch up.

"I didn't," Slocum said. "Pearlie did it for us."

The three men shared a smile.

"You think they'll find her?" Pearlie asked, oblivious to the men's conversation. "I'd sure hate for the wolves to get her tonight."

"We'll find her," Slocum said.

Then Pearlie stopped dead in her tracks thirty feet from tepee. "I can't go in there."

"Why not?" Slocum asked.

"There might be Injuns in there and they—well, you know what Injuns do to women."

"No. Not in this one. Blue Water is inside. Blue Water!" he called out.

"Yes?" She appeared.

"This is Pearlie, our new guest, and she is staying the night. Look after her." He frowned to emphasize his point.

"No Injun men in there?" Pearlie asked, still hesitant.

"No men, only you and me," Blue Water said, and guided her into the doorway. She looked back and nodded that she had the situation under control.

"Portugee John and his boy Beaver Tail will be here at dawn," Slocum said, seeing the column of troopers go over the rise to the west in the golden reflection of the low sun. "I want the best horses chosen and carefully packed. One sore back and we are out an animal."

Black Wolf nodded. "Everyone will work," the chief said.

Slocum acknowledged the man's words.

Bordeaux drew a deep breath and shook his head. "What else will happen?"

"I ain't sure, but I am anxious to get going. What about you, Black Wolf?"

"They have told me for years that white people are like ants back there."

"They are."

"I have seen the wagon trains. There are even more."

"Wagon trains are only the trickle of a big river," Slocum said.

"Good. I must see them."

Slocum considered the man. He had lived the wild life. At one time his people had thought they were the most powerful—God's chosen children. To fall from the grace of your god must be a bitter pill. *Yes. Black Wolf, you will see the many houses and places of the white man.*

Slocum considered the soft wind. Maybe the first day on the trail would be clear and not so bitter. He could hope so anyway.

12

Slocum woke in the night to hear Pearlie talking to herself. She lay in her blankets beyond the ring of the red coals. He lay awake and listened to her words.

"Are you there, Jed?" Then a silence. "Jed, don't tease me—I know you're out there. You've been naughty again, Jed. Haven't you? I know what you do in that shed. I know, Jed. You play with yourself, Jed—" Then she began to breathe regularly, and he knew she had fallen asleep. The warmth of Blue Water's body sought his back. He closed his eyes, laid his face upon his right arm, and tried to go back to sleep himself.

Jed was her brother's name. He recalled her saying it before on the trip to the fort with Black Wolf and himself. The chief thought demons possessed her. Superstition was a way of life for an Indian. Possessed individuals were held in special regard in Indian camps. He recalled one among the Cheyenne who dressed like a woman. He had pursued Slocum on several occasions. Luckily Slocum had managed to avoid him.

Then Slocum began to worry about the thirty packhorses. The thoughts made his stomach roil. Add in the saddle animals, and it would be a trek he would not soon forget. Best they head south to hit the Oregon Trail and then go east from there.

This was the last night for a while that they would spend

in the confines of Blue Water's snug tepee. He'd come to respect its sanctuary and warmth. At long last he fell into a troubled slumber.

Long before daybreak, Blue Water hugged him and he rolled over to face her. In an instant, her hungry mouth covered his and she sought him. Her rock-hard nipples drilled fiery holes in his chest. He quickly took her heat-radiating body into his arms. Her sweet musk filled his nostrils as they kissed.

At last, out of breath, they separated. In the dim light, he could see the glint of stars in her eyes. He closed his own eyes and savored her nearness for a moment longer. His hands filled with the muscled flesh of her butt; then he deeply inhaled. Time to get up and start preparations.

In a short while the camp came alive with activity in the predawn light. The breath of man and beast made great clouds. They began to fight the first war, to load everything up. Everyone worked. Men and boys were dragged around by roped horses plunging about. Squaws saddled the ones they could hold, and Jim brought out bales of the furs to load.

Slocum helped ear down a rambunctious gray pony. Black Wolf rushed up with a rope and formed a halter on his head. Then the two hung on to the lead rope as the pony lunged around them in a circle. Slocum couldn't find a place to dig his boot heels in the slickly packed snow. He and Black Wolf were soon being dragged further from the camp.

"Let go," Black Wolf shouted. "I will handle him."

"How can you if two can't?" Slocum strained on the rope, his soles finding little surface to stick to.

"You may get hurt," Wolf said, more insistent than before.

"What about you?" Slocum countered, not about to let go.

"I am a Sioux."

"So?"

The gray pony took to leaping in the air. At last, Slocum's boot heels stuck through the crust, and the two managed to twist the pony's head back far enough back that the animal threw himself on his side, flopping over. Like lightning, Wolf rushed in and sat down on his head.

"He will soon be tame," Black Wolf said, sounding satisfied

that the act of pinning the pony on the snow would the fight from him. "Must have gone wild after we put them out." It was a Sioux explanation for the pony's behavior.

"Good luck." Slocum tossed him the lead rope tail.

"You go check on the squaws. Be sure they do it right," Black Wolf said, straddling the horse's neck and head. The gray blew a roller out his nose, but remained pinned down despite his kicking fits. "The boys and I will get the horses."

Slocum moved on. Black Wolf had some purpose in all this; to keep Slocum out of any harm was what it looked like. He shook his head at the notion and went on. Spotting another wild one on a lariat, he moved into to help the boy on the rope's tail. The pony soon yielded, but not before Blue Water and two other women rushed over to help him.

Slocum began to feel there must be a conspiracy against him. Did they know something he didn't? Black Wolf's ways were one thing, but the entire band acted as though he needed to be coddled. He headed for the trading post, still confused by their concern.

Out in front, Wolf's lieutenants, Red Deer and Blue Fox, eared down a horse being packed. They each had a headlock on a piebald while women loaded the bales of furs. Slocum nodded his approval, taking a cup of coffee from Jeanne, who came outside with a shawl over her shoulders.

"It is going well," she said in approval.

"Yes. The sun isn't up and we're half loaded."

"I never saw so many Sioux working so hard at once," she said, looking around at the activity.

"They're pretty dedicated."

"They want those new repeaters Jim promised them."

"Oh." He had heard nothing about repeaters. Obviously, then, they wanted the trip to be a great success. It halfway explained why he was kept away from any danger. Even made some sense. What would Black Wolf and his men do with the long guns?

Hunt game and defend themselves? He hoped so, and moved in to assist two squaws trying to get a pannier on the cross-bucks. The pony moved about nervously whenever the weight of the bale touched him. With the pack hung on the cross-bucks, the animal let out a death scream and shot into the air.

Thrown backwards, Slocum landed sprawled on his back. He looked up into the anxious brown eyes of three Sioux women.

"I am fine." He sat up and shook his head. This mothering business was not going to get it done. He hurried to his feet, recovering his cap and beating the snow off it on his leg. With the cap set back on his head, he searched for the errant pony. Nothing in the dim light indicated where the bucker had gone.

"Some boys rode after it," Blue Water said, rushing to him out of breath. She looked him over. "You are all right?"

"I am fine," he said, not too gently.

"I was only concerned."

He regretted his sharpness, and forced a smile for her. No need to spoil their game. Besides, he considered Blue Water very sincere and he didn't want to sound unappreciative.

"It is going the way you want?" she asked.

"Yes. It is going good." Well enough, despite the few wild animals. He had expected worse from ponies driven in from the range.

"I will go help them." In a swirl of her long fringe, Blue Water was headed back to work. Absently he admired her shapely derriere under the leather.

"She's a very pretty girl," Jeanne said, standing beside him with a coffeepot and a new tin cup in her hand. "Have some more. You took a real spill."

"Nothing serious. Thanks. I wonder where the Portugee is at?"

"Listen for bells. He has sleigh bells on his big horses."

Slocum cradled the hot cup in his hands, and the warmth soon drew back the feeling in his fingers. All he could think about was San Antonio and how the warm winter sun would soon be up there. The early morning merchants would be out, like the milkman with his cart, peddling fresh milk from cans. Or the firewood peddler, his burros heavily laden with sticks for stoves, his shouting shattering the quiet. The tamale man would come heralding his wares. Donkeys would bray and the colorful fighting roosters would soon be trying to outdo each other, crowing from fence-high perches.

The nice thing about being in Texas instead of in Nebraska was that the sun would warm the air when it rose. In this white land of ice, its weak rays only reminded him how nice it would be to spend the afternoon on the patio of Estancio's cantina. To sip on wine or tequila and while away the evening, maybe watching some shapely señorita's dance on the flat rock floor.

"More coffee?" Jeanne asked, holding the pot up.

"Oh, yes."

"You are deep in thought?"

"Yes, ma'am. If it takes this long every day to get loaded, we won't get there in a year."

"I am sure it will smooth out."

"It will have to." He glanced down at the attractive woman. Jeanne was a rose in this out-of-the-way place. And a good person. Bordeaux was a lucky man. Slocum handed her back the cup.

"I better go to checking and see what we have left to do," he said, and started off.

The gray seam of the new day widened on the horizon. Off in the distance he could hear the bells. That must be Portugee John and his boy. Right on time.

13

Slocum looked back over the line of his train in the sparkling sunlight. A big dusty rose-colored Belgium with his head down pulled Portugee John's cart. The horse's great feathered feet churned up dusty snow. Still, he came with ease up the long slope. The next wagon in line, heaped with hay for the animals, was driven by the man's boy Beaver Tail. Next came Blue Water and the lead packhorse. Pearlie rode sidesaddle close by her. He felt grateful that Blue Water had a way with the girl. The long string of animals came behind them, with Owl Woman riding up and down, using a quirt on the resistant ponies to make them hurry and keep up.

One of Black Wolf's men led the five spare horses. Soon the Sioux chief drove his buffalo horse up to where Slocum sat his bay.

"The ponies are more settled," the chief said, acting satisfied.

"Yes, and need to be more so, or we will spend our days loading them."

"They will be. I know a place we can camp this afternoon." Black Wolf motioned his head to the south. "An old abandoned dugout we can sleep in."

"Good," Slocum agreed. The notion of shelter warmed him. Though he suspected the midday temperature had risen to twenty degrees, any warmth against the night's steep drop would be nice. Also, he had watched a high bank of clouds building in the west all day. They'd be lucky if they weren't in a blizzard by dawn.

"How far away is it?" Slocum felt uncertain about the chief's idea of what the horses could do in a single day and still last the whole trip. Indians had little respect for such things.

"We will be there long before dark," the chief said.

"Good enough. Is that snow out there?" Slocum asked.

"Could be," the chief said without even glancing in that direction. "I'll go check on that dugout?"

"Sure. Are we headed right to arrive there?"

"Go more—" He used his arm for a semaphore and Slocum saw the direction he meant, more left and southeast. With the sun out he didn't need it, but he did have a small compass in his pocket that he'd used when driving cattle. Three days of clouds and a man could get turned around fast. He watched Black Wolf gallop away on the powerful buffalo horse. He was a strange man who had been thrust into a new way of life—he had many hard days ahead.

Slocum booted his horse off the ridge to go speak to Portugee John, to tell him about the dugout and their plans. The train's situation looked peaceful enough. He hoped Black Wolf was right and things would go better.

Black Wolf loped the pony south. He liked the feel of the wind in his face. If only he had a buffalo to pursue. But he doubted they would see one. The only buffalo left were far to the west. Maybe, with their new rifles, they could get permission from the colonel to go out there and look for them. Perhaps there would be one more great hunt. From the first one killed, he would eat the heart and liver raw. Bordeaux might get them passes—Captain Brown would never allow them to do anything.

He swung down in the valley and studied the few bare cottonwoods along the creek line. This would not be such a bad place to camp, but if the dugout was there it would be warmer. He reined up the pony, slipped from his back, and took a hatchet. Certain no one was in sight, he stepped out on the ice and began to chip a hole. The horses would need water. If there was live water below, then Slocum could stop and let them drink here.

Soon water began to fill the hole he'd chipped out. Good, this would be the place to drink. He climbed the slick bank and stuck his ax in the scabbard on his saddle. In an instant he was on the pony and headed on his way. He crossed several sweeping basins and dropped down to the one where he expected to find the dugout.

How many years since he had found this place? Several, but it was well constructed and should still be sturdy. He had been en route to a horse raid far to the east. He had heard of the Pawnees' wonderful horses. He and a close friend, Green Shirt, had ridden many days to find those people who lived in great underground houses like prairie dogs. The two friends split up to search for them. Black Wolf discovered their women working corn in small plots under great trees along the river. On his belly in the bushes spying on them, Black Wolf wondered where Green Shirt had gone and if he'd found their horse herd.

Black Wolf could recall watching the bare-breasted squaws bent over, hoeing the weeds from their plants. They even used iron hoes. Well concealed, he grew hard from the sight of those Pawnee women. Especially one who was no doubt part Spanish. Her wide eyes looked like those of a doe. Such a slender nose—he wondered how she could even breathe.

At last he cleared his head. He wasn't there to screw their women. He had come to steal their best horses. He backed up like a snake until he was out of the women's vision and hearing. In his retreat, with the rich sour smell of the soil in his nose, he'd heard the scream of a proud stallion and hurried off to find his companion.

That would be his goal. Take the greatest breeder from them. The Pawnees he knew gelded their lesser-quality horses. He recalled once a Cheyenne had brought one such animal to trade. Being curious, he had inspected where the animal's testicles should have hung. Under close scrutiny he'd found only faint scars remained on the shriveled sack.

"They make squaws out of them," the Cheyenne had said in disgust to him.

Black Wolf recalled the warm summer sun on his back while he was lying and watching the young Pawnee boys herd the prize band. Green Shirt, at his elbow, was anxious to hear more about the Pawnee women he had seen back at the river.

He told him about the pretty one.

"Perhaps we can take her and the horses." Green Shirt grinned.

"They have only boys for warriors." He meant, of course, the boys herding the horses.

No, Black Wolf did not think they should try to do both. They were many moons from their own land. Their flight must be swift. A woman would only hinder their escape. He wanted one of those bald-faced stallion he had spotted with the herd. Even at that distance he could see the muscular ways of the studs. Breeding them with tough mustang mares would produce great buffalo horses.

Yes, the words were true about these people. The Pawnee were true breeders of horseflesh. Oh, how he felt great pangs of jealousy for their wealth of beautiful animals. This day he would possess at least one great stallion from that herd.

"What about the woman?" Green Shirt asked him again.

"Ah, we should think of horses, not women."

"She would make our nights shorter going back." His friend grinned foolishly, and Black Wolf could see his mind was set on kidnapping a woman.

"Do you worry more about your dick than the future of your people's horses?"

"What will one stallion do?" Green Shirt wrinkled his face in disgust at Black Wolf's notions.

"I want to take four."

"And this woman you speak of?" Green Shirt smiled like a foolish boy who would not be dissuaded from his desires.

"We must take her quickly," Black Wolf said. "Once they spread the alarm, the entire Pawnee nation will come after us."

"Ah, who cares. I can kill a dozen Pawnee."

Black Wolf considered the way they must do this. Despite Green Shirt's brave talk, Black Wolf knew the Pawnees would not sit by and let two young Sioux warriors steal their best horses and prettiest woman without pursuit.

"I will steal the horses," Black Wolf said. "You can grab the girl and we will meet in the west."

"But alone, how many horses can you steal?"

"One, perhaps two."

"But you wanted four."

"I cannot handle more than two alone. And you are so insistent on taking the woman." Black Wolf hoped his words would change his friend's notion about taking her. "Come," he said, easing backwards. "I will show her to you. Then you can decide if she is worth all the trouble it will cause."

"I want to return with a Pawnee slave so pretty that others would lust for her."

"I only want horses that can carry me faster to the hunt." What must he do to show his friend the foolishness of his purpose?

"Ah, but with rifles who needs such ponies?" Green Shirt made a face, then grabbed his breechclout and smiled.

Black Wolf wanted to tell him he would rather kill the buffalo with his own arrow while riding at a full gallop beside the lumbering animal. Not like some cowardly white man who would shoot it from afar. He regretted ever telling his friend about the beauty in the cornfield.

But he agreed to go back and spy on her for Green Shirt's satisfaction.

Loud crickets in the tree canopy made a hissing sound that hurt Black Wolf's ears. The two of them crept around briar brambles. Somewhere a red-tailed hawk screamed. He considered that a good omen. The voices of the women carried on the afternoon wind that rustled the cottonwood leaves. Birds sang over the two men, so Black Wolf knew they were blending well with the woods.

At last he saw her out in the field. She raised up from her hoeing, and her pear-shaped breasts trembled with firmness. Her rich brown skin shone with perspiration. He indicated her to Green Shirt.

The look on his friend's face told him enough. The best horses in all the world would not satisfy him now. Black Wolf dropped his gaze to study a black bug pulling an insect in its beak back to his den. The victim had green wings.

"I have seen a bad omen," he whispered. "We must go."

"I don't believe so. Go steal the horses that you want and I will take her and meet you in the west. Above the stage station where we camped."

Black Wolf could see the determination stamped on his friend's face. There was no way to change his mind. Black Wolf felt sick. There was nothing he could do but try to steal a stallion or two and then ride like the wind and later meet his friend.

"I will give a war cry when I take the horses, so you can hear me."

"Then I will take her."

"In two nights I will wait for you at the station." Black Wolf looked hard at his friend. The sight of the beetle dragging the green-winged bug away made him sick to his stomach. He rose up; he must try to steal some horses.

"Yes, I will be there," Green Shirt said, but he never looked at him.

Black Wolf drew a deep breath and eased himself out of the thicket. There were so many things he wanted to tell his friend, but more than that, he could not forget the black bug with the green one. He hoped his vision meant nothing. Yet, like a firebrand, it ate at his stomach.

He must pray to the Great Spirit for his friend's safety. Black Wolf would return in shame if anything happened to him. How could he face Green Shirt's family and tell them that like fools they had parted so close to such a large village.

Was his greed for the new bloodlines so great he was neglecting his blood brother? His heart heavy, Black Wolf mounted his pony and worked westward. Glancing back one last time at the thick woods, he skirted a tall grass meadow. Around the point where he would be unseen by the women, he crossed the stream and sent the pony up the hillside; he hoped to come out by the horse herd.

Soon he heard the sounds of the stallions' challenges. His heart quickened. Dismounting, he stripped down to his loincloth. He bundled his clothes and tied them on to his saddle, for he would need them later. Then he took his tomahawk free, set the bow over his head and the quiver in place on his back, and remounted.

Atop the ridge, he gave a great war cry that thundered across the prairie and headed for the horse herd. Several of the smaller boys fled in fear toward the smoke of their camp over the rise.

One of the youths chose to die, and came to meet him armed with a lance. They charged each other with the fury of conviction in both their hearts. Black Wolf felt the heat rise in his chest. They met, and came within inches of a collision, but the ponies half-stepped aside at the very last moment. Black Wolf deflected the spear, then drove his ax deep in the boy's chest. He lost his grip and saw the youth unhorsed and spread-eagled on his back.

With a bark of victory from his throat, he quickly searched about, seeing no one. Close to trembling with his excitement, he shook loose a leather lariat. By this time he realized there would be only a chance to take one of the stallions before the Pawnee poured out of their village in force. He pushed his pony after the great red and white painted stud. Powerful medicine made his lariat sing and his catch was good. His rope captured the great stallion.

When he rode in close, the one he now called Big Man danced and pranced. The stallion half-pawed at his horse, but the buffalo horse knew better and only snorted to warn his adversary. With little time to waste, Black Wolf reached out and fashioned a halter on the stallion's head.

Black Wolf turned and saw on the far horizon many Pawnees charging at him on horseback. This was the only stallion he could steal. He put heels to the buffalo horse and they went west. To his great relief, Big Man matched the pace.

Wind swept his face and the excitement of his coup made his heart beat hard. If his friend was so lucky, they would meet in two nights above the Platte River station. Nothing touched him but wind and the sweeping grass heads that brushed his knees.

Five nights he waited above the Platte. Black Wolf made much medicine. He did all he knew how to do for his friend, but Green Shirt never came. Empty-hearted at last, he rode back to his tribe, who were camped in the Black Hills. Once there, he gave Big Man to Green Shirt's family. He spent the summer burning sage and looking in the smoke for a vision of his friend.

Then, in the fall, a Cheyenne came among them, a man who traded with many tribes across the plains. A medicine man found Black Wolf in deep meditation away from the camp.

"There is a man here who trades with our women who knows of your friend."

"He knows about Green Shirt?" Black Wolf struggled to his feet in shock. He felt dizzy as he considered the news.

"Yes, and when you know the truth, you must stop fasting and go become a warrior again."

He listened to the older man's words and considered them.

"I will," he promised.

"Good. You saw what his fate would be and he never listened. You cannot save those who wish not to be saved."

"I understand." The man spoke the truth, and only then did Black Wolf realize what he meant about his friend's fate. The news would not be good.

"No, you don't understand. You have no idea the wonderful powers the Great Spirit has given you. Use it for your people," the old man said pointedly.

"I will. Where is this man?"

"In camp." The man made a face of disgust.

"I will do as you say, wise one. But first I must know the fate of my friend."

The wise one walked away. Black Wolf knew he'd heard his words. Yet he made no sign. Had Green Shirt died as a warrior? If his friend had gone that way, then he could go on with his life and do the things the wise one wished of him.

He hurried to the camp, where he found the Cheyenne trading with some women.

"You have been to the great house of the Pawnee?"

"Yes," the wrinkled-faced man said.

"You know of my friend Green Shirt?"

"Yes."

"Is he alive?"

"Half alive is all."

"Half alive?" He frowned at the trader's words.

"Yes, he is a slave of the Pawnee and they gelded him."

Black Wolf looked hard at this man in angry disbelief.

"It is not him!" It could not be his friend who stole horses with him from the Arapaho and Cheyenne. Who with him had scattered the Crow like they were the white man's chickens. This could not be him.

"Yes, it is. His name in Sioux is Green Shirt. He said he came from this band."

"Did he send word to me?"

"Yes. He said your medicine was strong and he was a fool to deny it."

Black Wolf closed his eyes. When he opened them again, the cloud bank in the west shrouded the sun. His world was stark white and cold. He pulled the blanket closer in front. No longer was he in summer, but riding the snow-clad grassland looking for the dugout.

At last he saw a patch of cedars and knew he was close. He crossed the ridge and soon spotted the closed door in the hillside. Good. They would have shelter.

He must ride back and tell Slocum. When he reined the buffalo pony around, he sniffed the wind. Slocum was right. It would soon snow.

14

Slocum wished the chief would return. The grass was enough out of the snow cover here that they wouldn't have to feed hay to the animals. The sun hung low in the west. They needed to make camp. With the cloud bank moving in, he wanted to be fortified someplace to sit out a blizzard if necessary. Where was Black Wolf anyway?

He rose in the stirrups and searched the horizon. The others were on his tracks. They'd managed to water the stock at the creek crossing he'd marked earlier for them. This place Black Wolf wanted them to camp at must be too far for one day's push. Indians had little respect for animals' ability to last, but Slocum had few extra horses and no plans to steal more from his enemies—the way a Sioux often did.

He rode back to Portugee John's wagon.

"I'm going to look for the chief. He should have come back. We need to make camp soon."

"Fine. I'll stop before dark if you aren't back."

"Good idea, but I better be back by then."

Slocum swung the bay out and loped off to the south. The horse was grain-hard from Bordeaux's generous care. Slocum made easy strides crossing the next ridge, and held him to a trot crossing the wide empty swale. How much further was it?

Then he saw a figure top the ridge. He looked familiar enough, and Slocum reined in the horse.

"How much farther?" he asked Black Wolf when he rode up.

"Over that rise."

"Got worried when you were gone so long."

"I went to visit some places from the past, and did not realize the time had passed swiftly."

Slocum accepted the man's word, and gave a glance back at the ridge. If the chief wanted to tell him what all that meant, he'd tell him. Slocum glanced again at the far heights; maybe they would make it over there by dark—he hoped so.

"It is still a good place to camp," Black Wolf said.

"Fine, we have gone too far today."

"It will make the horses easier to handle."

"Also weaker."

"Yes. Now I can smell the snow too."

"I told you about that this morning."

"You did." Then Black Wolf laughed aloud at his discovery. "Who is the medicine man here? You or me?"

"We both need to sharpen our skills."

"You ever know Sitting Bull?" Black Wolf asked.

"I seen him once at a treaty." Slocum rose in his stirrups to look for the train. They should be breaking over the ridge soon.

"He is a powerful man. He has seen much in his dreams."

"You are friends?"

Black Wolf shook his head. "No, Sitting Bull is by himself. Like many powerful, men, he lets no one influence him."

"Why is he in Canada then?"

"He hoped the queen mother would treat him better than the blue legs."

"Hoped?"

"Hoped."

The first wagon came over the rise. Slocum could hear the bells and nodded, pleased, then reined up his horse and looked back. So Sitting Bull's retreat to Canada had turned out well. Maybe Black Wolf would realize the way of peace was the only one. Perhaps he already knew. There was no telling about a man who had lived the free life; he always wanted to go back.

"Just over that rise?" Slocum asked again.

"It will be there."

Darkness set in while they unloaded. Everyone was weary, but they all laughed a lot. Owl Woman made a cooking fire from some cedar dragged in for her to use. The men and squaws unloaded packs. Slocum moved among them inspecting the horses' backs and withers for raw spots. He found one, and shared a look with Blue Water, who nodded.

"He will need a thicker pad tomorrow," he instructed her.

She acknowledged his words with a nod.

It was a busy time. Then he looked around. Where was Pearlie?

"Have you seen Pearlie?" he asked Blue Water. She blinked and shook her head.

"Black Wolf!" he shouted at the man. "Where has Pearlie gone to?"

Black Wolf struggled with a pack in his arms, and Red Deer moved in to help him set it down.

"I have not seen her."

"She was here when we stopped. She can't be far out there."

"I'll go look for her," Black Wolf said, and ran for his horse.

"I'll go—" Slocum said, but knew when he said it that the chief would rather scout for her than unload panniers.

"Be careful out there," Slocum said, catching up with him when he had mounted.

"I will be back."

Where had Pearlie gone? The light was shutting down fast. A few dry flakes danced in the air. Slocum hoped Black Wolf could find her tracks before total darkness set in.

"How did we lose her?" Blue Water asked him. "I only went to help unload. I told her to stay close."

"It wasn't your fault. We all must watch her." He realized they had been some time unloading and Pearlie might be miles from there.

"What is wrong?" Portugee John asked, the smell of liquor strong on his breath.

"Pearlie's wandered off and Black Wolf has gone to look for her."

•   •   •

Black Wolf soon took up her tracks. They headed eastward. He loped his pony hoping the light would last long enough for him to find her. Why did she ride away? No telling about a possessed person. The temperature was dropping.

If it grew cold enough, the new snow that fell would be very fine. He pushed the pony onward. Bent low, he held the blanket closed with one hand to stay warmer. The light grew dimmer in the ghostly world around him. No sign of her. He had expected to find her by this time. Still, her horse's tracks were in the snow. He narrowed his eyes.

Then he reined up at the sounds. It was a terrible mixture of noises, squeaks and shrill notes, like a dying animal made, but different. He halted his pony and progressed slowly. The sounds grew louder. Then he could heard the laughter of white men and voices. They were having a celebration. The sounds made him concerned for the crazy woman. He dismounted and ground-tied his pony.

His single-shot rifle in his hand, he stole to the crest of the hill and looked down into their camp. A great fire licked at the sky. Some men in buckskin danced to this squeaky music coming from something with sticks that the player held to his chest. Obviously they were drunk. Their shadows made them looked like giants on the sides of the canvas tops of the wagons. Where was Pearlie?

Perhaps he should go get Slocum. Slocum could talk to these men, and they would believe him that Pearlie was possessed and needed to join her own people. For Slocum they might give her up without a fight. Belly-down on the ground, he watched them cavort around. They were full of whiskey, and he knew what these men would do to her. The quicker he removed her the better.

First he must locate her horse. She would need it to ride back to camp. Their flight would need to be a swift one. Secondly, he must find her. Black Wolf took off, moving like a low shadow. He intended to come in behind their wagons and learn more.

The loud music continued. Black Wolf eased himself past the line of horses and mules. He found her horse still saddled. Then he squatted down and from underneath the wagons, observed the dancers by the fire. Satisfied they had no guards posted, he began to inspect the wagons.

"—hold still, girl. You're a little tight, but I'll get my root in yah."

Black Wolf froze in his tracks. He could hear some muffled protest in response to the man's words. Was the man talking to Pearlie? Black Wolf retraced his steps to the back of the wagon. By the firelight shining through the translucent canvas, he could see a big hairy butt. No doubt the man was trying to rape her.

If he killed this man, the others would seek revenge. They might charge the pack train, and that would endanger Slocum. Black Wolf needed to knock him out, if he could.

He discovered a shovel on the side of the wagon, and with care eased it out. Standing still, he listened to the man complain more about her tightness that he obviously could not penetrate. In a bound, Black Wolf was in the wagon.

"Who's there?" the man grumbled, but too late. The shovel was raised high, and rang like a bell on his head. Black Wolf struck him again to be certain he did not make another outcry. He looked into the wide eyes of Pearlie, who had scrambled out from under the man. Gagged by a kerchief, she looked shocked enough at Black Wolf that he wondered for a moment if she would even go with him.

In a fury she fought down her dress to cover her bare belly and legs. He felt helpless. The look on her face was enough to tell him she did not recognize him and considered him only another rapist.

"Come, we must go," he hissed at her.

She shook her head slowly, deep distrust written in her blank eyes.

"You through in there with her yet, Mike?" Someone beat on the wood sides of the wagon. Black Wolf regretted leaving his single-shot rifle on the ridge with his horse.

"Guess not—" The man's voice trailed off.

Black Wolf's breath came slower. He could only hope the man had given up. With his fingers, he gestured for her to come with him. If only the Spirit Woman would speak to her and tell her that he did not wish to poke her, only take her back to the others.

She reached up and pulled the gag from her mouth.

"I know you."

"Shush!" He held his hands over her mouth. If they didn't hear her, it was a wonder, but the music noise was still going on. He looked at the rear of the wagon. Nothing. But this horny bunch would not be long before coming to see about her.

"Come, we must go," he said.

She started to rise, and then began to crawl toward him. It eased his concern. He moved to the back to the wagon, then turned and looked back for her. She followed—thank goodness. He helped her down, hoping no one saw them.

Any second, he expected the two of them to be discovered. He guided her around the horses. Behind them, he stopped. She didn't have her blanket wrap, nor a coat. No time to go back. He wrapped her in his own blanket and shoved her toward her horse at the end of the line.

"Where is everyone?" she asked.

"We are going there." He led her to the stirrup.

"Get up," he said, and boosted her into the saddle. "We must ride hard."

"Which way? It is dark."

He glanced back at the sounds of the revelers.

"Follow me." He slipped in and took a saddle horse loose for himself, then cut the picket rope. If he scattered their horses, maybe he could divert their attention from him and her long enough for them to get away.

"Gawdamnit!" came a roar from the wagons.

Black Wolf let out a blood-curdling cry, and thirty head of half-asleep horses and mules plunged at the line. It gave, and they tore off to the east. He could hear the men's response to it. "Get them gawdamn horses!"

"Ride!" he shouted at her, herding her horse up the slope ahead of his. Halfway to his goal, he heard the pop of rifles behind them. Too far away, too dark to be accurate. He screamed at her to hurry. On top, he changed horses, swept up his rifle, and pointed westward into the inky night.

"Go!"

They tore off. He kept checking over his shoulder, but all he could see was the glow of the fire beyond the horizon. The noisy music had stopped too. There was just the drum of their horses' hooves on the thin snow. He drew a deep gasp of the frigid air. Without his blanket he would be very cold when he reached camp. Still, the crazy woman was safe and he was still alive.

15

Snow drifted down like feathers from a plucked chicken on the flames of the campfire. Hunched under several blankets, Black Wolf finished his story of Pearlie's rescue from the white men. The hot coffee Owl Woman brought him finally began to warm him and stopped his shivering.

"Who were these men?" Slocum asked.

"Hiders?" Black Wolf shrugged. He didn't know them. "They were dressed in buckskin and had four wagons." He frowned. Maybe someone knew about the noisy thing they played for music. "One man had a sack with sticks coming out of it. Went like this—*eee, oh.*"

"A Scottish bagpipe," Slocum said, amused, and shared a smile with Portugee John.

"I am not sure what it was. They danced to it." Black Wolf shook his head in disbelief. "Made plenty of noise or else I would not have gotten her away."

Everyone laughed.

"Me and Beaver Tail's turning in," Portugee John said, and motioned for the slip of a boy to get up. A look of reluctance crossed the youth's face; he obviously wanted to hear more of the adventure.

"Good night. Tomorrow will come soon enough," Slocum called after them. Blue Water returned and knelt beside him.

"She is asleep," she said, and indicated the dugout.

Slocum nodded. Pearlie's adventure would add nothing to her sanity, probably make her worse, though she had hardly spoken since Black Wolf brought her back. It had been a long day, and many more faced them. They needed to keep the girl under closer supervision. In her current state, she might do anything. He hoped trouble did not erupt with those hiders. The three Sioux and Portugee John could be counted on, but the five of them would be no match for a large force of well-armed buffalo hunters. Black Wolf had done the right thing taking coup on the man with the shovel. It left them less likely to want to avenge the attack. Amused, Slocum felt ready to bet it had nearly killed Black Wolf's old warrior soul to leave that man alive in the wagon.

He considered the falling flakes. If the snow kept up much longer, they might be forced to stay a day near this dugout.

"We will guard tonight," Black Wolf said, and motioned to his two men.

"I can do my part of it," Slocum volunteered.

Black Wolf shook his head. "Sleep means little to a Sioux."

"Here, you take this Winchester then. If you need me, I'll be inside." Slocum handed him the rifle, then rose to his feet under the blanket. The larger flakes settled on his shoulders like petals.

Black Wolf nodded in approval at the weapon.

Inside the dugout, the light from the fire shone in the open doorway. He found his and Blue Water's blankets. She was already under them. Beyond lay Pearlie, which made him feel easier. Unbelievable how she had slipped away that fast and gotten into that much trouble. It would be a cold night. He settled down fully dressed under the covers. Portugee John and his boy were in their bedrolls across the small room.

Slocum lay on his back and studied the dark log ceiling. Blue Water snuggled her back toward him. He patted her hip to acknowledge her presence and stared at the underside of the roof. Snow and trouble with hiders—what would happen next? It wouldn't be an uneventful journey. And Black Wolf took the lead every time. The chief had even run off to look for Pearlie. He handled the guard duty too with his men— why? So no harm would come to Slocum. It went back to those repeating rifles that Black Wolf must be counting on so much. Slocum felt grateful to Jeanne for telling him about them. It explained some of the things that had happened.

He rolled over, threw his arm across his woman, hugged her warmly, and shut his eyes. Sleep came.

Black Wolf sat on his haunches with the rifle across his legs. Snow swirled around him like moths at a light. The hiders would not venture out on such a night, not even for revenge. But he couldn't be certain, and he did not want the stock run off either. He could make out the outlines of the horses, huddled with their tails to the northwest wind. Every once in a while one would bite another and a scream of complaint would shatter the stillness of the night.

No doubt the approaching storm had upset the horses and that had caused all the troubles when they loaded them in the morning. Animals could always sense such changes even before they arrived. He had been so worried that Slocum would be injured, he had forgotten the signs that even the white man noticed.

He shifted his weight to his other leg. This trip would be made a day at a time. At that rate it would be long one. Despite his desire to hurry it, they would be perhaps three moons going to this place and then coming home.

What did lay ahead? *Oh, Great Spirit of the Sioux people, Buffalo Woman, come to me and show me the way I must be. The things I must do.* He closed his eyes in deep meditation. *If only she would come again and tell of the things ahead.*

Nothing moved in the night. One of the horses snorted. Where was she? If only he could bring her back. Then he saw the white buffalo bull emerge in a cool white light that looked like a tunnel in the snowy night. Black Wolf's heart stopped. The powerful one was coming. Skin crawled on his neck. He must be at peak alert, for he had not burned sagebrush to cleanse his earthly ways. Could this mean that he would be unacceptable for her to talk to?

His legs turned to stone, but to move or change his position might be seen as a weakness. No goddess wished to talk to a weakling coward who could not stand a small cramp in his leg.

Then she emerged in her elk-skin dress with the long fringes. As if sculpted from ice, she appeared frozen, but she moved with the grace of a very supple maiden. He felt only inches tall as he squatted on his haunches before her. How could he even dare be in her presence? He recalled that he was the one who'd asked for her. But he'd never expected her to return so soon.

"Go and sleep," she said in Sioux. "Your enemies are in their camp tonight."

"Will they come for us?"

"They are your enemies."

He nodded.

"There will be others. One will ride an Appaloosa horse with a blanket rump, and the ones you saw at the trading post. They are all your enemies, but tonight you may sleep."

"Will I be able to keep Slocum from harm?"

"That is your mission."

Why? Of course. The rifles. But why Slocum? He dared not broach the subject with her. These were her orders and he must obey or lose his place as the chosen one.

"You have done well," she said. "It is a difficult mission."

"Is this a test?" he asked, but realized that she was fading like dying light. He could see nothing, as if she'd walked through an opaque tapestry and evaporated. Then he heard the horses in the sifting snow. Short of breath and shaken, he stayed in one position for a long while to gather his senses. When he felt he understood all she'd told him, he rose to his feet and headed for the dugout.

Still shaken by her appearance, he went over her words. Difficult was a small word for his problems, but he knew the enemies—the hiders, the bunch of robbers, and a man on an Ap horse. Had she told him about all of them? There was no way to know when he would met them.

"What is wrong?" Owl Woman asked when he joined her under Portugee John's wagon. "You are trembling."

"The Great Spirit came to me again."

"Again? Tonight?"

"Yes, right out there. Before, when I called to her, she did not come—she must not have had anything to say. But she came tonight and warned me of more enemies who would keep us from getting these furs to Independence."

"Why are you shaking so then?"

He drew a deep breath to try to recover. "I am shaken by her presence."

"Oh, I worry for our people. But with her looking after us, maybe we can find a place in this new world of whites." She threw her arms around him and buried her face in his neck. He could feel her warm breath on his skin and felt better. She always improved his spirits at times like this in his life.

He wanted to tell her he still hoped for a place where they could hunt buffalo and live the good life, but he dared not raise her hopes. The Great Spirit had not promised him anything like that would happen. Perhaps next time he could be more specific with her about the future.

How long must he protect Slocum? He hugged Owl Woman tight. There were too many things that he did not know about in this new world that emerged around him. He was grateful Owl Woman had come with him. She was a very firm post to cling to in the vast prairie of nothing that surrounded them.

He thanked the Great Spirit for coming. It was very important he not appear ungrateful to her either. With Owl Woman in his arms, he watched the snowflakes swirl in under the cart where they lay beneath the robes and blankets. What next? He grinned at her when he felt Owl Woman's familiar fingers encircle his manhood.

Slocum awoke with Blue Water in his arms. Slowly he eased away and rose. But she quickly threw back the covers and rushed off to relieve herself. He moved about the camp, stiff from sleeping on the ground. It had been a restless night too— he had awakened and listened many times for sounds. The cold flakes melted on his face while Blue Water returned and built up the fire.

"Going to snow all day?" Portugee John asked, blinking his eyes and stretching his arms over his head.

"Might do it. I figure we better strike out. We won't get

there any other way. We have fodder for the horses."

"Ah, I guess so. I just hope we don't find those hiders and them mad at us about Black Wolf taking Pearlie from them."

"Hope not too," Slocum said. But if it happened, then the hiders would have to be dealt with. He would much rather not meet up with that bunch, but who knew anything about the future?

Black Wolf joined them and held out his hands to the fire.

"No one came last night?" Slocum asked him.

"No, only the snow and some wind."

"When we get loaded, why don't you ride ahead and scout us a way. We don't want to go too far today. We have to save the horses." Slocum looked hard at the chief. He wanted a commitment on that.

"Move to the southeast," Slocum said. Then he recalled the small compass in his pocket. He removed it and snapped open the lid. The needle danced around and pointed north.

He looked up. Black Wolf stood above him. Slocum made a semaphore sign with his arm to the southeast. "That's the way. You need this?"

Black Wolf considered it, chewed on his lower lip, and nodded. "Your magic is good too."

"It may take all the magic we've both got to get there," Slocum said, handing the compass to him.

Black Wolf studied it in his palm in the dim light. He whirled on his heels and quickly checked it again.

"You cannot fool it," Slocum said with a shake of his head. "And don't argue with it. It is always right."

"What is up there?" Black Wolf asked, looking northward.

"A strong medicine rock, they say."

"Must be a helluva mountain too," Portugee John added.

Black Wolf pocketed the silver case. Had such a force drawn Sitting Bull that way? It was good that he knew about such a powerful force and why it beckoned him. He must always be careful not to be drawn in that direction unless he intended to go that way.

Black Wolf felt anxious to be by himself and test the compass's power some more. Slocum had given him the magic, so he must trust him. Good. Before he left them, he would tell Red Deer and Blue Fox to watch out for his ward.

The sun would hide behind the clouds when it finally came up. But in his pocket was a gift better than his own sense of direction. *Don't argue with it.* The needle pointed north each time. Strange.

16

At midday, Slocum saw them coming. He rode from the center of the train toward Portugee John's place at the head of the train. At a shout he twisted in the saddle and spotted Blue Fox on his pony hurrying to join him. He was pointing to something coming off the rise to his right. There was no mistaking the brown-clothed figures even at the distance as they plowed snow coming toward the train. They were hiders or frontiersmen.

"Keep Pearlie on that side of the train," he told Blue Water while riding by the two of them.

"Whose that a-coming?" Pearlie asked as Blue Water took her bridle and led her to the other side of the line of pack-horses.

"Strangers," Blue Water said.

"It's them, ain't it?" Pearlie asked softly.

"We don't know," Blue Water said.

"Keep your shooting iron handy," Slocum said to Portugee John as he rode past him. "They might not want nothing. But you never know."

"I'll be ready," he said, and Slocum rode out from the train to meet the riders.

"What do they want?" Blue Fox asked, drawing his pony close to Slocum's stirrup.

"If it's the ones Black Wolf took her away from, they probably want her and the rest of the women with us."

"Will they want to fight?"

"Naw, they'll want to see how strong we are first."

Blue Fox nodded and booted his horse to keep up.

"When they see there's only four men in this outfit, they might try something. Here, take this Colt," Slocum said. He reached down and took the small Colt .30-caliber cap-and-ball from his right boot. He handed the gun to Blue Fox.

For a long moment, Blue Fox studied the handgun, then nodded in approval and stuck the revolver in his waistband.

"Be ready to use that gun at the first flinch they make." Slocum studied the riders on short ponies plunging forward. No telling if they were liquored up or just wandering around. But his experience with hiders told him they considered life a cheap commodity.

"Howdy," a big bearded man said, holding up his hand in the peace sign. The others drew up in a line beside him. A motley crew, Slocum decided. Unshaven, unbathed rowdies in smoky, grease-stained leather outfits.

"Howdy," Slocum offered, shifting the Winchester across his lap.

"Well, you're traveling with Injuns, I see," the big whiskered man said.

"You've got eyes. My name's Slocum, this is Blue Fox."

"Brackston's my name, that's McKey, and that's Buster, Frenchie, and Eddie."

"Good day, gentlemen."

"You got a white girl with you?" Brackston sneered toward the train.

"What about her?" Slocum demanded.

"She's my wife and some gawdamn red nigger stole her from me."

"You better look again. You are mistaken. She was given to my care by Captain Brown of Fort Robinson to deliver to her family in eastern Nebraska."

"I say—"

"Brackston, she's a ward of the U.S. Army and you better keep your pecker in your pants. Army finds out you been raping their wards, you might get your neck stretched."

"Who said I raped her?" His face grew black with anger.

"I said if you try."

"Where's that buck hit me over the head with damn shovel last night?"

"He ain't here, but he'll be back—" Slocum saw the man on the end move. In an instant, Slocum filled his hand with the .45 from his holster. With the hammer cocked, he was ready.

"You try and pull that gun, I'll blow you off that horse, mister."

"What is this?" Brackston demanded. "All we want's that crazy girl. We'll take her and leave you and these red bastards alone."

"You aren't taking nothing. Turn your butts around and ride. I'll shoot first next time."

'You're making a big mistake, Slocum, or whoever you are. I'll get that woman and finish what I started. Won't be no damn red nigger take her away from me the next time either." Brackston reined his horse around hard.

"Come on, boys, let's go. This bastard's going to see what we're all about before this is over."

Satisfied they were leaving, Slocum holstered his Colt. He watched them ride into a wall of snow to the northwest. He turned his horse around to head back to the train stretched across the white prairie in a long line.

"They'll be back," he said, and Blue Fox agreed. They reached the train, and Blue Fox went to join Red Deer and tell him about the men.

"Big trouble, huh?" Portugee John said, and spat tobacco on the ground. "I saw where you had your gun out."

"Yeah, man named Brackston wants Pearlie or else."

"Or else what?"

Slocum cast a glance northward; they were long gone over the rise.

"Or else I'll kill him, I guess."

Black Wolf studied the trees from afar. Huge gnarled cottonwood trunks lined the banks of the frozen stream. Before he booted his horse toward them, he wanted to be certain they were not hiding an ambusher or a camp of some more stray white men. Those were always the most desperate kind.

He felt uncertain, but booted his horse ahead. Nothing looked out of place, but he could feel the skin crawl on his neck. He shifted the repeater across his lap and set it butt-down on his leg so he would be ready—in case.

Ravens called off in the distance. The snow here was shallow, and his horse soon trotted toward the trees. Maybe he had become too cautious, afraid of his own reflection in the water. No way to know. Traveling in such cold and snow was not a sane thing to do. Still, for each man in his tribe to own rifles like this one—he had done worse things for much less.

He rode under the huge cottonwood. The wind sifted some snow off a higher branch. It drifted down, chilling his face with the icy spray. Then from out of nowhere a lariat encircled him and he felt himself ripped off his horse.

A trap. He'd fallen into a trap.

"Give me that damn rifle!"

Black Wolf stared up into the colorless, scarred eyeball of One-Eyed Jacks and the muzzle of his cap-and-ball pistol. The walnut stock of the repeater was wrenched from his grasp; he managed to sit up on the icy snow. He could smell the man's strong breath, and wondered how many others he had with him.

"Where's that pack train at?"

"What pack train?" Wolf asked in Sioux.

Jacks slapped him with his hat.

"Damn you! You better talk English, you red bastard."

"Many tepees come," Black Wolf said, and tossed his head west. His plan was to convince Jacks that there were more Indians coming.

"I seen your bunch at Bordeaux's." Jacks spat close by his leg, then wiped his mouth on a ragged sleeve. "Why, you ain't got enough damn bucks to make a full circle." Stiffly Jacks rose up straight. The kid moved in and bound Black Wolf's hands behind his back with rawhide.

"Now, where are they?" Jacks demanded.

"Over the hill," Black Wolf said, hoping to figure out a way to escape them before the train arrived.

"Boys, I reckon all we've got to do now is wait right here and let that Slocum bring us them furs." Jacks cackled, and his laughter caused chills to run down the side of Black Wolf's face.

The Great Spirit had warned him of his enemies. How could he be so stupid? They'd lain in wait for him and he'd ridden right into their trap. No fire, no smoke. Somehow he must warn Slocum and the others. Seated on the cold ground with his hands tied behind his back, he realized there was little he could do.

Jacks had gone over to talk to the other two out of his hearing. No doubt, from their hard looks back at him, they were making plans for the ambush. Slocum would be coming down his tracks. Maybe Slocum would scout ahead and he could signal him in time. So far, they had not tied his feet. Perhaps when the time came, he could get up, run out, and warn them.

Many things rushed through his mind. The close calls he'd had in the past with the Crows and the Pawnees. He was lucky, for only a white man would have captured and tied him up. His other enemies would have struck him dead by this time or tortured him.

Maybe they had such plans. The wind was sharp without his blanket. He'd lost it in the fall from his horse. Where had his war horse gone? He tried to look around for it. The gray was not in sight.

Strange. The buffalo horse would usually stay close when he dismounted. Perhaps going off over his butt had startled the animal. Had the horse spooked and run away? No telling. Black Wolf flexed his sore wrists; the rawhide cut into the skin. Luckily it was cold, or the ties would have shrunk more. He hoped they would stretch; they were stiff as it was.

Slocum blinked in disbelief. The proud gray horse came churning toward them in a spray of snow. His head high and mane unfurled, he screamed with a stallion's authority. Then he dropped his head as if satisfied, and ambled up to the train, which had stopped for lunch.

"That's the chief's horse," Portugee John said.

"I can see it is." What did that mean?

Owl Woman rushed out and brought the stallion to Slocum. There was concern written on her face.

"It's his pony, all right," Slocum said. "What do you figure?"

"Something's wrong. He's been shot or something," Owl Woman said as the others pressed in closer for a look at the hard-breathing pony. "This horse would never leave him on foot."

"I better go see about him," Slocum said, handing Blue Water the bowl of dried buffalo stew.

"I will go," Blue Fox said.

"No, you better stay here. Them hiders might come back while I am gone."

Blue Fox and Red Deer agreed.

Blue Water came over and spoke to him while he tightened his cinch. "You must be careful, my man."

"I will. He's probably fine. May have fell off his horse." He laughed, saw her concern, and became serious again.

He placed his arm on her shoulders and pulled her closer. "We get this job done, we may go off in the mountains somewhere and spend the summer together. I know of places."

"I could show you such places too."

"You be thinking about them places. I'll be back quicklike, and you will see Black Wolf will be all right." He kissed her hard on the mouth and when he finished, he saw his impulsiveness had embarrassed her—kissing her in front of the others.

He mounted up and sent his horse off in a long lope, spraying powder over himself and the pony. Black Wolf's safety was foremost in his mind. What kind of trouble could he get into out here? The hiders were northeast—at least they'd ridden off that way. Slocum pushed the pony harder. His problems never ended on this job.

17

Slocum blinked his eyes in disbelief. The chief staggered out of the treeline ahead with his hands behind him. They were shooting at him. Puffs of gun smoke were swept away by the wind. Whoever was cutting all the caps at Black Wolf meant business. Then he saw Black Wolf go down in the snow. Damn, they'd shot him. Slocum spurred his horse at them with his own Colt in hand. The three figures began to blast away at him. The range was too far and he held his own fire. He decided they couldn't hit a bull in the ass and would soon be out of ammo.

"Jacks, you one-eyed bastard!" he shouted when he recognized the ringleader. "You better throw your hands up! Or I'm coming to kill you!"

He took aim off the plunging deck of his pony. In rhythm with the horse's rocking gait, he sent his first shot close enough that snow showered over the trio. The kid broke and ran. The old man threw his gun down, and Jacks ran for cover.

Slocum frowned as the form of Black Wolf came rushing over and bulldozed the old man off his feet. The chief must not be badly hit. Slocum reined up his horse and jumped down.

"Try something, you're dead," he warned the bewildered-looking old man, whose hands were in the air.

"The rifle," the chief shouted, and indicated the tree where

113

it was propped. Slocum could not see the other two. No doubt they had found their horses and fled. He ran over and swept up the long gun. There was no sight of the other two, though he could hear the strain of leather and the pounding of hooves.

Black Wolf fell back on his butt out of breath.

"They get the jump on you?" Slocum asked.

"Sure did. Drug me off the gray."

"The gray came and told us," Slocum said.

"Good thing he did."

"Yes, I would say so." Slocum turned and appraised the old man. "What have you got to say for yourself?"

"You ain't the law," the surly outlaw said.

Slocum kicked him out flat on the snow. "I did that for Pearlie, you grubby bastard. You're going to find out who's the law."

"Get on your belly," Black Wolf ordered, and stepped in and tied him up. "You watch him," the chief said, straightening up from his chore.

"No. This time I am going after them. You keep the old man."

"What will we do with them?"

"Give them over to the authorities in Ogallala."

"What will they do?"

"I'd bet they have plenty of wants and warrants on them three besides robbing Bordeaux's." Slocum stepped in the stirrup, made two hitches at getting up, and on the second one made it. "Put them away in prison for a long time."

How long did he dare leave the pack train alone? Those two couldn't go far. He searched about, but didn't see them, then nodded to Black Wolf and set out on the kid's tracks, which wound under the trees along the creek bank.

Be lucky if he didn't get ambushed himself, although they'd hardly had time to reload their cap-and-ball pistols. Last he saw of the kid, he was hightailing it like a wild man. Pistol grips in his hand, Slocum booted the horse onward. He was ready for anything.

Then he spotted the kid looking back over his shoulder and running away on foot. Slocum booted the horse into a lope, and soon rode up until he was right on heels of the wide-eyed outlaw. With his right foot out of the stirrup, he gave a hard shove in the center of the upper back that sent the kid rolling end over end in the snow.

Slocum reined up the hard-breathing horse and brought him around.

"On your feet, stupid, and you can run back to camp, you're so all-fired head up about running."

"I ain't, mister, I swear I ain't."

"You should have thought about that before you took us on."

"I never—"

"Get to running or I'll drag you on the end of my lariat at a run."

"I'm going. Honest—I'm winded."

"Get to running. Faster," Slocum shouted. "Go faster!" He closed in on the kid with his horse, his patience worn thin with his pimple-faced captive. He hated the fact that Jacks had escaped. He would be harder to retrieve. Maybe he and Black Wolf should consider giving up the notion of a chase and get back to the train. Portugee John and the others could never hold off those hiders if they tried to take Pearlie back.

He frowned when he spotted the dark spot on Black Wolf's shoulder.

"They've shot you," Slocum said with a scowl.

Black Wolf made a face to dismiss his injury.

"We better get you back to camp."

"What about them?"

"I'm figuring." He knew the chief wanted the pair dead.

"Get on my horse. No telling where their horses are at. We need to get back to the train and see about that shoulder."

Black Wolf obeyed, but Slocum noted he held his right arm when in the saddle. Slocum herded his prisoners with an eye out for Jacks. He marched them along until they topped the hill, where he could make out the wagons coming toward them.

Red Deer and Blue Fox rode out to meet them. Black Wolf spoke to them in Sioux. They took the prisoners and gave Slocum one of their mounts. He waved Black Wolf to go ahead, and leaped on the pony's back.

How bad was the chief hurt? Black Wolf was tough, but lead bullets could stop elephants too.

"What is wrong?" Portugee John asked.

"Black Wolf took a slug. We better hold up and see how bad it is."

"Who shot him?"

"One-Eyed Jacks. We got his gang."

Portugee John lost no time stopping and tying off his reins. He bounded to the ground and reached back for a canvas ground sheet.

Black Wolf dismounted and shook his head to dismiss the men's concern. By then Blue Water, Pearlie, and Owl Woman were there.

"Build a fire," Slocum told Owl Woman.

She slipped off her horse and came running. She spoke in Sioux to Black Wolf, and then she inspected the wound with a wry look.

"Must not be deep," Slocum said to reassure her. "Lots of times the powder is bad and the bullet has no power." He couldn't imagine Black Wolf hit hard and still walking around, but there was no telling about the man. He was plenty tough.

The chief took a seat on the blanket. He acted very unconcerned. Owl Woman began to undress him. Portugee John gave him a small crock jug of whiskey, and everyone cheered him on to take a drink.

Slocum sat on his haunches and studied the bleeding hole. Not a .44-sized wound. More like .30-caliber. Blood ran down Black Wolf's muscular back from the wound on his shoulder blade.

"How will the bullet come out?" Blue Water asked, crowding in close.

"If it isn't deep I can do it with my jackknife," Slocum said. He did not like his own surgical skills, but they appeared to be the only ones at hand.

"The fire is started," Owl Woman said.

"Good. I'll need to heat my knife. That's suppose to stop an infection."

She nodded.

"Oh, he's going to die!" Pearlie said, and clasped her hands over her mouth. "I just know it. I know it. He was a nice man too."

"Take her away," Slocum said to Blue Water. "I know it's not her fault, but she is upsetting."

"Oh, don't let him die. Please don't let him die—" Blue Water quickly ushered Pearlie around the other side of Portugee John's wagon while talking softly to her.

"Hope she don't know something we don't," Black Wolf said over his shoulder.

"She don't—just rambling. You better lay face-down," Slocum said to him. "Put some whiskey on a rag and give it to me."

Blood still oozed from the wound. Slocum carefully wiped around it with the rag. The only sounds were the horses blowing and snorting. Then he finished and rose to his feet.

"Be right back. Portugee, hold this rag on him."

Slocum went to the small fire and tested the jackknife blade on the hair on the back of his hand. It seemed sharp enough. Squatted on his heels, he held the blade over the low flames. The steel blackened and he rose, satisfied it was the best he could do.

"This will hurt," he said to the man lying face-down.

"Hurry, I am cold."

"Get some gunpowder," Slocum said to Portugee John.

The man nodded and went for some. Slocum looked at Black Wolf's two lieutenants.

"Hold him still."

They moved to obey. With both of Black Wolf's arms pinned down, Slocum bent over and probed with the knife blade. He soon found the hard ball. Good, it had not penetrated his shoulder blade. Driven in by force, the bullet was packed hard in the tissue. He had to cut enough around it to loosen the lead sphere and flip it out with his knife point.

It sounded easy, but the job required the skills of a surgeon, not a man who'd only watched such field operations performed. He felt Black Wolf flinch when the point of his instrument scraped over the bullet. Slocum's fingers cramped as he probed around the edge. He hoped it *was* the edge and he wasn't merely cutting the man's muscle fibers apart.

Then he tried to pry the bullet loose. It would not give. Blood continued to flow, and began to dry on Slocum's fingers. He pried again, and finally felt the bullet give. In a few long seconds it emerged coated with scarlet, and Slocum examined it between his fingers.

"Here's the bullet." He showed it to Black Wolf, who only barely shook his head.

"The next part will hurt," Slocum warned him. "I have to burn the wound out with gunpowder. It will sear off the bleeding and keep down any infection." He waited for Black Wolf's answer. The treatment would be severe, but it could save his life.

"Do it," Black Wolf said, his face buried in the canvas.

Slocum exchanged looks with Portugee John. The man shook his head gravely in disapproval and handed him a powder horn. With fingers drained of their strength, Slocum poured the black grains into the wound until they made a small mound mixed with blood. He shared an unspoken moment with the two men holding his patient down.

"A lucifer?" he asked.

Portugee John produced one for him. Slocum handed the horn back and took the match. This would be pure hell, even for a tough Sioux. The two had Black Wolf pinned down, but even they would not be ready for this test.

"Turn away," he said to them. They obeyed, twisting their heads aside.

He struck the lucifer on his gun butt, then touched off the powder. The flash was blinding. A large white cloud of sulphurous smoke rose in the air.

Black Wolf gave a great grunt and then settled back facedown. The fumes ran up Slocum's nose as he studied the small blackened hole. No blood seeped out. Good. He would need bandages to cover it.

"He should be fine," Slocum said to Red Deer and Blue Fox. Both men nodded and released Black Wolf.

"Put a blanket over him," he said to the blanched-faced Owl Woman.

She quickly spread a five-point over him. Slocum wiped the blade of his jackknife on his pants. The concern now was whether Black Wolf would develop an infection.

"What else?" Portugee John asked.

"We need some bandages. Clean white cloth is best."

"We haven't got any of that, have we?"

"Yes, we do. Pearlie's petticoats. Those fort women washed her outfit before they sent her. I noticed."

"How we going to talk her out of them?"

"We ain't. Blue Water can do that."

Portugee John looked toward the wagon that concealed the two woman and shrugged. "Good luck."

"I'm going to need lots of it," Slocum said, and rose wearily to his feet. With the chief recovering, they were down to four fighting men. If those hiders ever learned that, they'd be back for the women and the furs.

A cold shiver of realization shook his shoulders as he looked at the two dull-eyed prisoners. One-Eyed Jacks was out there somewhere in the snow too.

18

The restriction of the bandages was the first thing he felt when he awoke. On further inspection he discovered his upper body was bound up tight in a white cloth. Black Wolf realized the hot spear in his right shoulder was from the wound. Groggy from the whiskey, he rolled onto his left side and found the heat-radiating form of Owl Woman beside him.

He could make out a thousand stars overhead. In a great yawn, he half-raised and searched about. The fire was down to red ashes. He needed to get up and relieve his bladder. With a dread for the cold, he rose and with a single blanket over his shoulders, went around behind the wagon.

His breath came out in small puffs of steam. Beyond the rig, he stood in the stark white night and pissed on the snow. Slocum had removed the bullet. He'd even shown it to him. But somehow this was not the reason that the Great Spirit had told him to protect this man.

Out there somewhere was the answer. The spirits had chosen him to go on. His shoulder would heal. Crow arrows had not killed him. He still had one of their arrowheads in his leg. Soon after he'd received the wound, his leg had grown sore, red, and swollen, and for days his fever had run high. Then a medicine man had drawn the poison out with the liver of an antelope and other herbs he gave him to take. In a few days, Wolf had been well enough to hunt again.

Strange that he'd never considered Slocum a medicine man. Perhaps white men did not brag about such skills. But Black Wolf knew a doctor from the fort—Slocum didn't act like him either. Black Wolf must learn how the man did the operation. The fire he'd made in his shoulder hurt the worst, but it must be part of the magic.

He soon found the warm form of Owl Woman under the covers and cuddled to her. It was good to take her along. Many nights on the warpath, sleeping alone, he'd wished he had her warmth to share. He soon fell back asleep despite the hurting.

By dawn they were packed and Blue Fox saddled his horse for him. The two white prisoners were told to ride with them— he heard Slocum warn them if they tried anything they would be killed. Good. They knew the rules. Though Black Wolf considered turning them over to authorities a waste. Nothing would be done to them. Better their carcasses fed the magpies and ravens than waste food on them. But Slocum did make them help pack. And they scurried about, no doubt fearing the wrath of the big man. The notion caused Black Wolf to smile to himself—Slocum was a good ally, much better than him being an enemy.

The next days passed uneventfully. The weather turned mild and the temperature eased upward, fueled by a south wind. They reached Ogallala and turned the two outlaws over to the sheriff, a large man with a black beard and beady eyes who kept looking at Black Wolf and the others as if he wanted to kill them.

"Will he turn them loose?" Black Wolf asked Slocum outside the store where some young white boys loaded sacks of corn to feed the horses on the squaw man's wagon.

"No. They will spend much time in jail for what they did."

"Why did these people look so hard at me?"

"They have not seen many Sioux down this far."

Black Wolf acted as if that was enough of an answer.

Feeding the horses corn each night had given them much strength. Even his own buffalo horse was acting like he did in the springtime when the grass grew strong enough go on a hunt. Strange to feed such food to animals. More white man's ways. He must trade for some corn next winter and feed their special horses. The white man wished the Sioux to grow corn. He had not listened before to such talk, but there were many things to learn from whites.

He watched Pearlie talking to one of the white boys who worked at this place. What would she tell him? That the wolves would get her chickens if he didn't put them inside for her? Maybe about that yellow and white calf? She could do it so innocently that the poor boy probably believed her.

How come the hider had not been able to rape her? Black Wolf recalled the man's frustration and strange words. Perhaps she was deformed down there the way she was in her mind— he knew less about white women than he did about their men.

Long ago, he'd even spied on wagon train women. They'd bathed in the river with their clothes on. He had seen them in the Platte. It was as if nudity would kill them. Was that why their skin was so white? He wasn't certain, but white women, even crazy ones, stayed in their clothing all the time. Even Pearlie had to ride way off and be alone to relieve herself. Who would look at her if she did it beside the trail? If someone did see her privates, what was the loss? And why waste so much time and energy to hide from others? It was a natural thing for Indians to relieve themselves and not make a big issue out of it.

A black sergeant in uniform came across the street, and Black Wolf heard him speak to Slocum.

"Them's reservation Injuns, sah?"

"Yes, they have passes from Fort Robinson," Slocum explained.

"Them's Sioux, ain't they?"

"Yes, they are. That's Black Wolf, he's a chief."

"I just be checking is all, sah."

"That's your job. They have passes."

"Oh, yes, sah. Them three be at the Little Big Horn, you reckon?"

"May have been, I never asked them. I am taking these furs east for Jim Bordeaux, and they are some of his customers who are helping me."

"Yes, sah. Yous have a good day."

"I will, Sergeant."

Black Wolf rode over to where the line of their packhorses stood hip-shot in the street. He felt anxious in all the traffic. Teamsters driving double-wagon hitches of oxen went past them. Six yokes of oxen strained to move the heavy loads up ruts mixed with mud and snow.

He could see the hatred in the white men's eyes directed at him and the others. Their whips cracking and the teamsters' cursing at their charges made the steers speed up into a jog.

"Get out of the road, you gawdamn blanket-asses!" someone shouted. Black Wolf frowned and reined his horse around to find the coarse-voiced person. There was room to go around them.

Then out of nowhere, Slocum bounded off the porch, his foot struck the hitch rack, and next he landed in the saddle. The bay bolted forward and the loudmouth driver's mouth made a big O as he faced Slocum's .44.

"Mister, if you can't guide them mules around my pack string, then get off and lead them around," he ordered.

The man paled and drew in his lines. Black Wolf watched the black-bearded man's face swell up, and soon he retched over the side of his wagon. He had swallowed his chewing tobacco.

Black Wolf and Slocum shared a small grin.

"We better get going," Slocum said under his breath, and holstered his Colt. "We are wearing out our welcome here."

Black Wolf agreed. Better to leave this place before they had a real fight. Still, he felt a certain Slocum could handle several men at once, but this was not Black Wolf's kind of personal warfare. He watched the coughing mule skinner drive his double-hitch around them. But not without threatening looks at him and the others.

Slocum rode over and accepted the bill from the store clerk. He paid him, and Portugee John came out on the porch. He and the boy carried several whiskey jugs. Black Wolf knew he drank much each day.

They set up along the frozen Platte. The ice was thick and it required an ax to open a hole to water the stock. They watered the horses two at a time. Black Wolf stood by Portugee John's wagon. A bullet slapped into the wood sides and he hit the ground flat.

The distant report told him the shooter was far away. Slocum came running in zigzag fashion across the snow, giving orders for everyone to take cover and get down. He tackled Pearlie, who stood looking blankly at their efforts to find cover.

"Where is he?" Slocum asked, looking up from over her form.

Black Wolf motioned to the south, trying to pick out any detail from where the muzzle smoke had erupted and blown away. The shooter had been on top of the brown bluffs. No telling if he had stayed there or had gone on after taking his shot.

"Blue Fox, get on a horse and skirt around. Take my Winchester," Slocum said, and pressed the confused-looking Pearlie's head down. "It's by my saddle. And Blue Fox—you don't have to bring him back alive."

The Indian nodded. He shared a look with Black Wolf too, then set out on a low run, picked up the weapon, and was aboard his horse in an instant.

"Get behind the wagon. We can water the horses later," Slocum said. "Everyone get back of the water—Beaver Tail!" he shouted at Portugee John's boy. "That horse won't go no—"

The shot rang out and the thin youth's arms flew skyward. Black Wolf spotted the distant puff of smoke torn away by the wind. He rushed to join Slocum, and they quickly dragged the limp body of the boy behind the wagon.

"You tried to stop him," Portugee John said to Slocum, and dropped to his knees.

The gaping wound in the youth's chest told the story for Black Wolf. Even Slocum's skills could not save this one. He had died like a warrior—unafraid. His mother could be proud—sad, but she could take strength that her son had died in battle unafraid. The Great Spirit would receive him with open arms. He'd gone like a Sioux was supposed to die. Like so many of his people had gone—without fear.

"I hope Blue Fox doesn't get shot for his efforts," Slocum said softly, and glanced to the south.

"He is warrior," Black Wolf said to reassure him.

"Yes. But somehow I figured that shooter'd only take one potshot and then run—damn, I never thought he'd kill a boy."

"See why we never leave an enemy alive?" Black Wolf looked over and watched Slocum nod his head. Maybe this white man would learn about enemies. They were much better dead. Black Wolf hoped he would now know this for his own good.

19

Slocum felt relieved when he spotted Blue Fox returning in the twilight. They had buried Beaver Tail's body in the grove of trees. Portugee John chose to go off and drink away his sorrows by himself. Slocum could understand; the man was very private in his ways. The whole trip, he'd hardly spoken to anyone and kept to himself. The loss of his eldest son had to be painful, for he had chosen the boy to make this trip as his first adventure. Instead he'd been cut down by a ruthless assassin's bullet. Probably with a Sharps buffalo gun, considering the distance.

Slocum was joined by Black Wolf. Blue Fox dismounted and handed back the Winchester. He shook his head. Nothing.

"Any tracks?" Black Wolf asked.

"Yes, but he rode fast."

"Which way?" Slocum asked.

Blue Fox pointed east. Slocum shook his head. They were headed east too.

"I will ride the bluffs," Black Wolf announced. "My wound heals."

"We can talk about that in the morning." Then Slocum said to Blue Fox, "Get some food. Thanks anyway."

Slocum set up guard shifts. They had slept several nights without any, but the attack and loss of the boy made him antsy enough to be more cautious. He took the first shift, and was

126

seated in the shadows of the huge gnarled cottonwoods when he saw a silhouette of person sneaking up on the camp.

He rose from the ground and moved catlike to the next trunk. The starlight on the snow was enough illumination, and when the individual moved again, Slocum saw him. Bareheaded? He really expected him to be wearing a cap or hat. Slocum eased around the tree and headed for another, closer tree to hide behind.

He could hear the intruder's hard breathing and footfalls on the packed snow. He was only a few yards away. Slocum eased the Colt out and drew the hammer back. Then he twisted around to watch the intruder pass.

"Hands high!"

"Oh!" cried the person. "I'm not a robber!"

"Then who the hell are you?" Slocum searched him for weapons, but found none.

"Brad Compton. I come to see Pearlie was all."

"You what?"

"Is everything all right?" Portugee John came in his night-cap with his pistol in hand.

"Fine. Go back to bed. This boy here came looking for Pearlie." Slocum shook his head in disbelief.

"I talked to her in town today," Compton said. "She's sure pretty."

"She may be that, but she's a little—" What could he say to the boy? She was crazy or out of her mind?

"Well," Slocum began, "she's asleep. You better go home before your folks miss you."

"I don't have none. They all died of cholera two years ago. I ain't got nobody. Get to work, ah, little at odd jobs is all. Like, ah, loading that corn today."

"How old are you?"

"Seventeen, I guess."

"You ain't sure of that?" he asked, amused, holstering his Colt.

"No, sir, not really, but it ain't important, is it? I can work."

"Can you drive a horse?"

"I done it before. I ain't real special at it, but I swear I done it."

"I believe you. You have any duds and a bedroll back there?" Slocum motioned toward town.

"Rags and sacks is all."

"Nothing you want to keep?" He frowned at the boy's answer. Surely he had some personal things of his own.

"Mister, I ain't had nothing since they died. I wandered off to find a preacher to bury them right, and while I was gone someone stole everything—wagon, team."

"Two years ago?"

"Yes."

"We'll see in the morning if you can drive a horse. Now about this Pearlie thing. She is a ward of the Army and we promised to protect her. That means you can't spend all your time trying to court her."

He'd swear the boy blushed.

"I won't, sir."

"That understood, I want you to get some sleep. We have to move on come daylight."

"Where we going?"

"Independence."

"I've been there."

"Good." Slocum went to the wagon and drew out a blanket.

"We found another driver for your other wagon," he announced to Portugee John. "I'm taking some blankets for him to sleep under." Beaver Tail didn't need them anymore.

The man grunted sleepily in approval.

After Red Deer replaced him on guard duty, Slocum joined Blue Water in their bedroll.

"What did this one want?" she whispered.

"He's in love with Pearlie."

"She won't even know he's here."

"Shush. By the time he learns that, we'll have him driving the other cart."

She giggled and hugged him. "You are some man. He is in love with her?"

"That's what he said."

"But she is possessed."

"Hell, he may be too. He's an orphan. Destitute. Has no one either. Folks all died, wagon and team stolen."

"You are a good man." She kissed him good night.

He took a deep breath. He was crazy too for ever taking on this job.

They broke camp at daylight. Brad drove the second horse and cart. He had turned red-faced when Slocum asked him if he had spoken to Pearlie that morning.

"No, sir. I ain't itching to make the Army mad."

Slocum wrestled with telling the boy that talking with Pearlie was all right, but decided he'd learn that soon enough. They needed his driving skills worse than Pearlie needed a suitor. Anyone who couldn't drive the big gentle Belgium horse in the shafts wouldn't work for them anyhow.

Brad proved his mettle. He drove out behind Portugee John, and Slocum saluted him. Pearlie rode behind with Blue Water and the train was moving at last. Slocum glanced to the south—earlier he'd sent Black Wolf out scouting to be certain they had no more surprise ambushes ahead.

From the corner of his eye he noticed the black dirt mound of Beaver Tail's grave. It was a sad place for Portugee John to leave him. Slocum could imagine how the poor man would have to explain their son's death to his Sioux wife—that would be the hard part. Maybe they could find the killer. If anyone could locate a track, Black Wolf could do that for them.

It could be Jacks, or one of those disgruntled hiders, or simply someone who hated Indians. He had seen enough prejudiced looks from the people in Ogallala to know how much many of them hated Indians—good, bad, or indifferent, they disliked them for the color of their skin.

Some had their own bad experiences with redmen; others fed off the lies and distorted tales about the Indians. There were always those bullies on the frontier who took their pleasure out of gut-shooting dogs and the like. They'd rather make someone suffer and hear them cry than anything else. Those were the real dangerous ones. This shooter might be one of them—but at the range he suspected a buffalo hunter with a Sharps .50-caliber.

Perhaps his concern for Black Wolf adjusting to white

man's ways was less important than the problem of white men getting along with Black Wolf and his people. No easy task.

He looked over at Brad. He held the big Belgium right in where he belonged, and the pride shone on his beardless smooth face.

"I'll be fine, Mr. Slocum." Brad kept his gaze ahead and held the reins up as if ready for any move the well-trained horse might make.

"Good," Slocum said, and rode back toward Blue Water and Pearlie at the head of the long string of loaded horses.

"He is a good driver," Blue Water said, motioning toward the cart.

"He may make it," Slocum said, absently looking over the string.

"They are fine. No new sores," she said to assure him.

"We have to plow the garden soon," Pearlie said, riding up. "I'm ready for some fresh vegetables."

"We will, won't we?" Slocum said, nodded to Blue Water, and rode on back to check with Blue Fox and Red Deer, who were bringing up the rear with the handful of extra horses.

"I'll ride ahead and find a farm that has fodder for sale. There isn't much here for the horses to eat," he informed the two. "Keep a close eye out for that shooter. I know Black Wolf is up there, but the bastard still might try again."

They nodded.

"We will watch for him," Blue Fox said.

Out of habit, Slocum surveyed the distant line of snow-capped brown bluffs across the frozen Platte. He wondered what Black Wolf had found up there, if anything. Was the chief up to the exertion of being a scout? He didn't need to reopen that wound. But there'd been no infection yet. Maybe it would heal. He hoped so, and turned his horse to go tell Portugee John of his plans.

Then Slocum short-loped the bay away from the train. The sun tried to heat up the white world and the glare was blinding. Ruts in the road grew deep and forced him to rein the bay to the side. At last, he dropped him down in a trot and stood in the stirrups. He needed to get several hours ahead to pick a place that had feed and shelter for the night.

Past noontime he rode toward some haystacks and a low-walled cabin. Smoke curled into the clear sky, and a couple of dogs ran out to bark at him. A thin woman in her thirties came to the door; she only opened it halfway and eyed him sharply.

"Yes?"

"Ma'am, my name's Slocum." He removed his cap for her and dismounted. "I have a pack train coming this way and I need to buy some fodder for them for the night."

"My man ain't here right now."

"I can pay cash for the feed."

"How much?"

"I have about thirty head of horses to feed and could pay a dollar for their hay."

"Don't sound like much to pay."

"Dollar and a half?"

"I guess I could do that. Pay me." She held out her hand.

He paid her in coins, replaced his cap, and thanked her before remounting. She drew back her shoulders.

"Be seeing you later today," he said, and remounted, satisfied the ponies would fill their bellies at her stacks.

"Yes," she said stiffly.

He reined off the horse and headed back for the train. He'd been gone long enough. Strange, he didn't even know her name. She obviously was reluctant to deal with him without her man there. If it had been a man he'd dealt with, Slocum would never have paid the extra fifty cents. A dollar would have been a fair price for the night's fodder. Money on the frontier was scarce, and few folks saw any hard coins during an entire year, so his first cash offer would have been adequate.

He met up with the train at their noonday break. They had broken the ice in the edge of the river to water the animals. Everything looked all right when he dismounted and studied the bluffs. He wondered about Black Wolf and what he'd found.

20

Black Wolf reined up his buffalo horse. He leaned over and distinguished the tracks left by Blue Fox on his return to camp. He also noted in the snow the crooked hind foot on the shooter's horse. Blue Fox had spoken of it. The horse made a strange track, one hind hoof making a more sideways imprint. It was an easy print to follow. But Blue Fox, Black Wolf decided, was right. The man had traveled fast after the ambush. Blue Fox's decision to return to camp was a wise one. But the shooter would not suspect anyone trailing him this long after the murder.

Would the assassin strike again or had he gone for more help? This particular horse was not at Jacks's camp when they took him captive, or Black Wolf would have remembered seeing this print. No way to know if Jacks had taken a new horse, or if it was one of those hiders seeking revenge for Black Wolf's attack on them. He had hoped that bunch was still out in western Nebraska with their wagons.

He pushed his pony on at a steady trot. Squinting against the blinding glare off the snow, he wondered who he followed. His shoulder felt deeply sore, but he ignored the pain. Better he thought about their enemies than his own self. Perhaps he could have a vision of the man.

What had the Great Spirit said? His adversaries were the hiders and Jacks. She'd never mentioned any others. He found where the man had stopped to relieve himself, sometime in the night. The yellow stains were still obvious on the white drift. He must have a den somewhere ahead, for he rode like a man with a plan.

Black Wolf spotted smoke and drew up his horse. It came from in the brakes, out of a canyon. It might be the shooter's place. He followed the tracks further, but decided the rider had not gone toward where the obvious signs of life were. He had ridden around the place. Perhaps Black Wolf should detour and see who camped there; maybe they had seen the rider go by.

With care, he rode off the rim, using the bushy cedars for his cover, and spied on the camp deep in the cut. He considered the several crude lodges along a small water source fed by a spring. It was a poor Indian camp. He could see some half-naked brown children running about, and an old squaw carrying a large load of sticks for firewood on her back. He wondered what tribe they belonged to.

Satisfied they held little threat, he remounted and sent the buffalo horse downhill, alert for the first sign of defense, but saw no one. At last a child spotted him and sounded the alarm. Soon others came outside wrapped in tattered blankets to shade their eyes with their hands and stare at this lone warrior.

They must be Pawnee. He checked the horse to make him walk more slowly, and carefully eyed the women and old men. Then a large-framed man with his white hair in braids stepped forward and spoke to him in Sioux. "My brother, at long last you have come to my camp."

"Green Shirt?" he asked in disbelief. Could this be his long-lost brother he had not seen in twenty winters? He looked so old. Was it him?

"It is I."

"But I thought they—"

"They spared my life," he said, and nodded as if that was enough.

Black Wolf drew a deep breath. That summer day in the woods became so vivid—the dark beetle with the green-winged insect in its pincers. The ominous sign he'd seen that day, knowing in his heart that it had come from the Great

Spirit to warn him. Yet neither of them had heeded it, and this was the result. He shuddered to think of the pain his friend must have endured when they slit his sack open and removed the seeds of his manhood. A shiver of cold went through his shoulders.

"Come, my brother, sit in my lodge and we will talk of old times." Green Shirt indicated the hide-covered entrance.

"I search for a killer who shot and killed a boy last night in our camp. He rode by above here."

Green Shirt shook his head. "I know of no one passing here."

"No, he avoided your camp. I saw his tracks. He rides a horse with a crooked foot."

"Back foot?"

"Yes. You know the horse and who owns him?"

"He belongs to Brackston. A trader."

"He's from around here?" Black Wolf recognized the name. He was the one he didn't kill. If he had only cut his throat while he fumbled around on top of Pearlie. His white-man plan had not worked in the end—Sioux ways would have been much better.

"Where can I find him?"

"Come in my lodge, we must smoke. Then I can show you his trading post."

Black Wolf dismounted and handed the rein to a young boy. He carried the Winchester that Slocum had entrusted to him into the lodge. He did not know who to trust here; even his long-lost brother was suspect. The rifle was only on loan and belonged to Slocum. He felt better with it close by.

They took seats, and a handsome small woman fed the fire and nodded to him.

"You recognize her?" Green Shirt asked him.

"No." Black Wolf searched his mind, but the female was unfamiliar.

"She was the corn grower we watched that day."

"I thought—"

"Her man died a few years ago and she came to live with me," Green Shirt said, and smiled with pride.

Black Wolf nodded. So in the end he had her for himself. What a price to pay.

"They say you work with Sitting Bull?" Green Shirt asked.

"I was with him before the battle at Sweet Grass."

"That must have been a big day."

"It was a hot day. So hot your blood would boil sitting in camp. The dust was so bad it covered everything, burned your eyes, nose, and chest, but it was a bad day too."

"Bad day. I have heard many say it showed them."

"Showed them what?" Black Wolf dropped his gaze to the ring of rocks. "That Sioux could go live in Canada? Or that we could go live with Red Cloud like sheep on a reservation? No, my brother, the glory was gone by the next day and we moved away."

"What will you do?"

Black Wolf wanted to say when he was armed and his men were armed with new repeaters, then perhaps they would die like men or turn the whites back. He felt uncertain which way it would go. The Great Spirit hadn't told him how, so he dared not broach the matter with Green Shirt.

"I have searched for the vision, but it has not come."

"They say you made much medicine with Sitting Bull."

"Some. He is a lone man. He shares some things. Others he does not tell, even to the ones who work with him."

"I hear gossip he wants to return. The queen is not so good."

"Things have changed since he left. He will find the blue legs will not treat him any better. You could come join us. We are at Red Cloud's Agency, but I never see the old chief."

"It is good to talk in the Sioux tongue. I am surprised I can, for I have not spoken it much in many years. But no, my place is here with the Pawnee. I have been one of them longer than anything else. Besides, my woman likes it here."

"Do you get allotments?"

"Some."

"Do they demand a head count of the men?"

Green Shirt shook his head. "Pawnees have not caused any fighting. They have accepted the white man taking their rich farmland, cutting down their trees, and telling them to go west or to the Indian lands in the south."

Black Wolf nodded. They'd not only taken his balls away, they'd taken his will to fight, to be a man. Their whole meeting in this rickety lodge, his woman in rags and him too, made Black Wolf's belly queasy. Would that be his people's fate? Better to die like a warrior than suffer with this low place in life. It resolved his purpose. Get the rifles and by then the vision of what he must do would be obvious.

"Can you lead me to this Brackston?" Black Wolf asked, anxious to get back to the train. He could let nothing happen to Slocum. He needed those rifles Bordeaux promised him.

"Yes."

"Is it far?"

"A few hours."

"Does he have many men there?"

"No, they are out west hunting buffalo. He was too."

"I think he came back." Black Wolf decided not to tell him of hitting the man over the head with the shovel to recover the crazy one.

"Let us smoke a pipe first," Green Shirt said, as if stalling for him to stay longer.

Black Wolf agreed. Green Shirt could save him from walking in on the man. Better to go slow and let Green Shirt show him his man, despite his gnawing concern to get back to the pack train. Black Wolf watched him fill the clay pipe with shredded tobacco. He hoped the pipe would taste as good as he expected.

Green Shirt lit the bowl from a flaming stick the woman handed him. Then, after some short puffs, he passed the pipe to Black Wolf. He accepted it and nodded to both of them. The hot smoke filled his mouth and the bitterness dug into his tongue. He fought back the urge to cough. Bad stuff. What did this Sioux-turned-Pawnee smoke anyway?

He managed to suppress his dislike and handed the pipe to back.

"It has been many winters since we smoked together," Green Shirt said. "Are there buffalos left?"

"Some further west, but they are few."

Green Shirt nodded, taking deliberate puffs on the stem.

Small clouds of smoke leaked from between his brown lips. Black Wolf decided his friend enjoyed the terrible mixture. He could only hope that he didn't ask him to smoke more of it, for he could not think of a kind way to refuse his old friend.

At last, the smoking over, they rose and went outside. Black Wolf realized there were no horses in camp. What would Green Shirt ride?

"You have a horse?" he asked with a pained frown.

"No," Green Shirt said. "But I can run beside yours."

"Where are the Pawnee's horses?" He could recall their greatness—the wonderful paint stallion he'd stolen that fateful day long ago had left his imprint on many colts. Where had their animals gone?

"We ate ours." Green Shirt's gaze meet his eyes in understanding silence.

He would ride slowly. To not have food, to live in rags, sleep in flimsy hovels in such an insignificant place, and then to have eaten all their horses—he would commit suicide before he was lowered to such behavior.

"I know you do not approve," Green Shirt said, walking alongside his horse.

"Approve? I do not have to approve of you."

"Yes, but were I a whole man, I would have gone back to our people."

"You would have been welcome."

"I could never have taken a wife. Had children. Here I am accepted and Dark Eyes shares my blankets."

"Can you?" Black Wolf spoke his thoughts out loud, then regretted them.

"No, but there are other ways to please a woman."

Black Wolf avoided looking at him. He checked the dancing pony, who did not understand why he must walk so slowly. The white men's corn made him very lively. Black Wolf must remember that.

"This place where we go, it is well guarded?"

"Against the Pawnee?" Green Shirt laughed out loud. "Do you worry about chickens biting you?"

"Good." Perhaps they could ride in close enough for him

to kill the man, then return to the pack train. He looked across the empty frozen prairie, grateful for the afternoon sun's warmth. For many years, he had wondered, and at last knew the truth of his friend's fate. Better to have died.

21

Slocum rode out in front of the train. The bells of Portugee John's harness rang out. The man had barely spoken all day, and Slocum understood his grief. Brad drove the second wagon well. During the noon break, the boy had engaged Pearlie in some form of conversation about a rooster she was worried about. Her favorite one too. Red tail feathers and a golden body. Slocum had heard most of the girl's speech. She wanted Brad to save the rooster from the coyotes.

Slocum guessed Brad was so moon-eyed over her, he believed it all. He was beginning to think Brad intended to do something about her too. The boy wasn't stupid, but somehow Pearlie totally captivated him. Slocum could not figure out why. Maybe he should ask him when they made camp later on.

When they reached the small ranch, the shadows were long. Slocum rode up to the low-walled log house and dismounted, removing his hat. The woman barely opened the door.

"We are fixing to camp," he said.

"I see that. Well, you paid for it. Go ahead. You've certainly got several horses." She made a wry, disgusted scowl. "Guess you told me."

"I paid you twice the going rate."

"The others were too damn cheap. Good day. Oh, close the gates when you leave."

Slocum blinked when she shut the door on him. He heard the bar slapped in place. She'd said all she was going to. Where was her man? He mounted the bay and started across the snowy ground. Then he noticed three even mounds under the white snow. Graves. He guided his horse around them and the spindly cottonwoods that were planted around her yard. He would bet her man was never coming home again.

What had killed her family? It was tough to be a woman out there all alone. He used his callused palm to wipe his mouth, and considered the trials the woman must have experienced. *They were too cheap.* Those were her words about the price for her hay. Maybe life itself was too cheap.

"Someone live there?" Blue Water asked with a frown when he joined her.

"A very sad white woman."

"No family?"

"I think they all died."

"From what?"

He shook his head and busied himself undoing his latigoes. Concerned for the woman's plight, he had no answer for Blue Water. He gazed across the flat valley at the low-walled cabin. Then he lifted the saddle off the bay's back. The warm heat from the saddle pad swept his face and the horse smell curled up his nose.

"We better get unpacked," he said with a smile for Blue Water.

"Yes. I was thinking about the sad woman."

"I don't know. You can go speak to her later."

"Would she talk to a squaw?"

"Maybe. Say, where is Pearlie?" He whirled around.

"She was here a minute ago." Blue Water took off running to the other side of Portugee John's cart.

Slocum hurried to where Brad was undoing the draft horse. "You seen Pearlie?"

"Sure. She went to see that lady about her pig." Brad bent his head toward the house.

"What damn pig?"

"The one she imagined got out today."

Imagined? He stopped and looked at the youth, who was

busy hanging up the hames on the harness with care. Brad knew she talked in riddles. He might be smitten, but he knew Pearlie wasn't right, and still—well, damn.

"Blue Water! She's gone to tell the lady at the house about her pig that got loose."

"What should I do?"

"Go and see about her. Don't hurry back unless the lady doesn't want you. We can unpack."

"Yes," she said, and in a flurry of her fringe ran toward the cabin.

Slocum turned and studied the snow-covered ridge to the north in the twilight. Where was Black Wolf and why wasn't he back? It just gave Slocum more damn things to fret about.

"That woman won't hurt her, will she?" Brad asked, hanging his harness on the cart.

"No, she's either closed the door in her face like she did to me, or invited her inside." He turned to glance toward the house. Blue Water was out of sight too. He hoped the woman would let her in. Blue Water spoke excellent English; it would be a shame if the woman turned her away. But he also knew many settlers' distrust of all Indians ran deep.

He hurried off to help Owl Woman, Blue Fox, and Red Deer unload. It relieved him to see the hungry horses busy chomping on the sweet-smelling hay in the racks. Gaunt as they were, they might need to stay an extra day and recover some. It would cost him another dollar and half, but it would be worth it.

"Where did the women go?" Blue Fox asked.

"To the cabin to visit the woman there."

"Oh," Blue Fox said, but Slocum knew as he finished the last pack saddle that the Sioux had other things on his mind.

"You are worried about Black Wolf?" he asked.

"He has been gone all day."

"He told me he felt strong enough."

"Maybe I should go see about him."

Slocum looked around. That should be no problem. The pens of stout lodge poles would contain the horses if they were raided. Blue Fox could not expect to find much in the darkness, but who was Slocum to say he couldn't. He nodded his approval.

"Be sure and return," he said to the man.

"I understand." The tall Sioux ran off to get his horse and tell Red Deer he was going to look for Black Wolf.

Bent over her fire, Owl Woman looked toward the cabin. "They all right?"

Slocum followed her gaze. "Yes. I figure she lost her family sometime back."

The woman shrugged. He doubted she understood a lot of English. But she too was worried about Black Wolf not returning to camp. Maybe Blue Fox could find him. No telling what was keeping the man. Black Wolf had a mind of his own. What were his words that day? "I visited some places from the past, and that's why I'm late." No telling how the man's mind worked. Slocum felt grateful for one thing. Black Wolf was on his side this time.

He patted Owl Woman on the shoulder. "Black Wolf will return, all right."

She nodded and busied herself over her pots and kettles. Slocum went to find Portugee John, whom he had not seen in some time.

"There you are," he said, and dropped to his haunches. Portugee John only nodded and lifted the crock jug to take a deep swallow from the neck. Seated on a robe spread under him, with his back to the cart's wheel, he held a far-away look in his eyes.

"Not much a man can say when he loses his best friend or son," Slocum observed.

"No," Portugee John agreed. He snuffed his nose, then wiped it on his leather sleeve.

"I want you to know—"

"Not your fault. You couldn't do anything more."

"I could have stopped the shooter."

"You aren't God." Portugee John studied the crock jug in his lap. "I'm being paid back."

"For what?" Slocum shifted his weight to his other leg.

"Long ago." He shook his head slightly and was silent. Then

he drank more whiskey and wiped his mouth again. "The nightmares never go away, do they?"

Slocum agreed. The nightmares never went away. He heard Blue Water and Pearlie's voices. They were returning. Soon, in the last of twilight, he saw them crossing the open ground together. Slocum rose to his feet. Portugee John would soon be drunk enough not to care about the loss of his boy.

"I'll send some food over," Slocum said. "Be sure and eat. You will need your strength."

"Who cares?" he said offhandedly.

"We all do. Black Wolf is out there looking for that killer right now. Blue Fox went to find him. They'll both find him."

Portugee John nodded.

"You can drink yourself to Hell and gone, it won't bring him back," Slocum said in disgust. But his threat never reached the man. No one could reach him. He would be a drunk forever unless he ran out of whiskey and soon.

In the past, Slocum had seen men fall into a bottle and never come out. Portugee John was close to doing that to himself. Slocum's visions of good men ending up in rags begging for their drinks made him sick to his stomach. He moved to join Blue Water at the fire.

"Did you meet the woman?"

"Mrs. Van Dam. Her husband is buried there and so are her two sons."

"What killed them?"

"Outlaws, she said."

"She know their names?"

Blue Water shook her head. "The man with one eye—she told me about him."

"Jacks. Did the old man and boy we took to Ogallala answer her description?"

"She remembered Jacks. He raped her. So did the boy. Maybe more." Blue Water shrugged her shoulders.

"How long ago?"

"Maybe three moons."

"You tell her that boy who raped her is in jail?"

Blue Water shook her head. "By then Pearlie was busy talking about her garden and the weeds."

"Did the lady understand about her?"

"Yes. She smiled at her stories. Pearlie brought her something she needed. She laughed."

"Good. I'll go see her in the morning about us staying here another day. The horses need the rest. Besides, Blue Fox has gone to find the chief. No telling when they will return."

He glanced around and saw Pearlie talking to Brad. The look of pleasure written on the boy's fresh face was enough to reassure him. He knew all about her strange ways, and strangely enough was not put off by them.

Slocum stared out into the starlit night. Where was Black Wolf? Now he had sent Blue Fox off to find him. He hoped they both returned soon. More than anything he wanted this trip over. Deep in his belly, his sixth sense warned him his troubles were far from over and Independence was a long ways away.

22

Bellied down on his blanket, Black Wolf studied the yellow light emitting from the narrow window in the front of the cabin. A sod roof hung off the edges of the low eaves. There were two horses and a mule in the corral. Curs came out and barked in the night, then hurried back for the security of the porch.

"I could eat one of those," Green Shirt said from beside him. "I have not had good dog in a long time."

"Before we leave we will eat one of them," Black Wolf promised him.

"Pawnees don't eat dog."

"Tonight you are a Sioux."

"They eat dogs." In a throaty chuckle, Green Shirt acted amused.

"Does he have a woman in there?"

"She's Cheyenne."

"Will she fight us?"

Green Shirt shook his head. "I don't know."

"Consider her a warrior then."

"Yes. How will we take them?"

"I am thinking of a way."

"No hurry. I have not been a warrior since that sunny day we lay on our bellies in the woods and I lusted so much for Dark Eyes."

145

"Did you sleep with her before they captured you?"

Green Shirt shook his head. "Some things were not to be."

Black Wolf wished he had not asked him such a thing. He did not need to know such details. They'd parted as friends with different missions. He'd waited five days for him. He could never have sneaked into the Pawnee camp and taken his friend from their hands. Chances were he would have been too late to save him anyway. They probably were swift in their surgery.

"I thought I had escaped them that night," Green Shirt said. "My horse was tired, so I hid in some dense brambles. I tied her up so she could not escape, and closed my eyes for only a minute. I was so tired. When I awoke—they had me. Six Pawnees." Green Shirt looked away into the starlit night.

"They were very angry over the loss of their great stallion," he said.

"I gave him to your family."

"You did not have to do that. I would not have given her to your people."

Wolf stared hard at the outpost. Soon he must finish this business and return to the train. Slocum would be concerned over his long absence.

"They cut me that night," Green Shirt.

"I have shared your pain."

"No man can do that. But I am certain you have."

"I have since the Cheyenne trader came and told me what happened to you." Black Wolf rose, taking the rifle. "We have wasted enough time." He did not wish to hear more of the operation, nor of Green Shirt's suffering. If he woke up without his balls, he would have taken his own life, but everyone is different.

He moved down the hill listening to the barking of the dogs. If Brackston knew the sounds of his dogs, then he would not be upset at their barking. They only barked at the wind or some coyote yapping off in the south. Good enough reason.

"I will silence the dogs," Green Shirt offered.

"How?"

"I have ways." In a low crouch and holding his tattered blanket around him, he hurried downhill.

In short while Black Wolf heard a short yelp, then another. Good. Green Shirt must be dispatching them. Black Wolf drew in a deep breath of cold air. His moccasin soles crunched on the refrozen snow as he approached the structure.

On the small porch, he noticed one cur lying on his side dead still. For a long moment he tried to hear voices from inside. He had to know where they were so when he went inside, he could quickly kill them. A board creaked under his foot when he stepped to get closer. With his ear pressed to the door, he listened closely.

Inside a man coughed. It came from the back of the cabin. That might give Brackston a chance to duck his bullets if there was much furniture inside. Still, he must act quickly.

Green Shirt came around the corner carrying a small dead dog by his hind legs. In the starlight, Black Wolf could see his big grin. Supper.

"Gawdamnit!" someone in a gruff voice swore. "Bring me that whiskey."

Wolf cocked the rifle and motioned for Green Shirt to pull the leather drawstring. Satisfied the bar on the inside was past the catch, he used his foot to smash the door open. From deep in his throat came his most blood-curdling war cry. The rifle flew to his shoulder. There in the center of the room stood the same whiskered man that he had struck over the head with the shovel in the wagon. The man recognized him—for a brief second Brackston's eyes widened in disbelief.

The rifle smoked death. The woman screamed and screamed. Through the fog of spent powder Black Wolf watched Brackston crumble into a pile. In an instant, Black Wolf was upon the man. His hunting knife's polished blade glistened in the lamplight. He grasped the man's greasy hair. The razor edge slipped over the skull bone, and soon a great patch of his scalp came loose with a sucking nose.

"Ah!" Black Wolf cried, staring at the bloody trophy in his fist, and then let go with a warbled cry of victory. He had avenged the boy's death. His enemy was dead and scalped. His medicine was strong. Looking around, he saw Green Shirt struggling with the woman. He started across the room. In the old days, they would have taken turns raping her—but he could not offend his friend; besides, his own urge was no longer as great. That was for virile young studs on the war path.

"He's dead," he said to her.

She stopped fighting and dropped her head. He nodded at Green Shirt. It would be all right to turn her loose.

"She can fix the dogs for us to eat," Green Shirt said.

"Yes, she can do that."

"You hear him?" Green Shirt demanded in her face. "I'll go get them. We want dog, you understand?"

If she heard him, she never acknowledged it. But Black Wolf knew the woman would obey them. She had no choice but to serve them. He watched Green Shirt go out the door and reappear with two of the dead curs, one in each hand, a short-legged, fat black one and the other a sleek-coated yellow one. They would make good stew.

Green Shirt held them up to her, and without a word she took them. Her thin shoulders dropped from the weight of them as she moved toward the fireplace with the crackling wood fire. Black Wolf went outside, checked around in the night, saw nothing, and then came back inside the cabin's warm interior.

The woman had skinned the black dog and was working on the yellow one. He could see the large kettle over the flames heating water to cook them. He guessed her to be in her late teens. Most Cheyenne women were good-looking. He had seen many of them who made his guts roil to think about them in his blankets. Her figure did not look bad in her beaded deerskin dress. She was smaller than most Cheyenne women. She ignored the two of them as she worked.

Soon she had the other carcass skinned and began to butcher them, cutting them up and tossing the pink meat parts into the water. Saliva flowed into his mouth at the thought of this delicacy. A victory feast, and with his long-lost brother Green Shirts. This was how it should have been for years—the two of them on raids. He could use many things from this trading post, but had no way to carry them back to his people.

When they left they must burn this place. So nothing was

left for anyone, especially for Brackston's men, when they returned.

"Can the Pawnees use these goods?" Black Wolf motioned around the room.

Green Shirt shook his head. "The Army would blame them for his death if they found them in our camp."

"But he needed to be killed." Anger rang in Black Wolf's voice.

Green Shirt shook his head. "He needed to be killed, but he was white and we are red. The white man does not understand."

"I understand there are fine blankets here, and your camp— even you are in rags." He waved at the stock.

"We have no arms to fight the Army. And I do not wish to sit in a log jail all year. No heat in winter. They put chains on you and the iron will freeze to your skin." Green Shirt bared his wrists and showed the scars on his forearms.

Black Wolf nodded. He saw the marks. Rising to his feet, he strode back and forth across the room and tried to think out the matter. Here were many blankets, much food, supplies, and leather goods for the mere taking. In a few hours he would have to burn and waste all of them, yet his friend would not take a thing for his own poor people.

Green Shirt had only been a Sioux again for a short while. He'd returned quickly to being like his adopted people. This trader had killed a boy—he'd deserved to die. Black Wolf had followed his tracks above the bluffs to this place. No, he did not understand his old friend's ways. There was such a great need for all this in Green Shirt's camp, even more than among his own people back at Fort Robinson.

The water was slow to boil. He considered the Cheyenne woman squatting beside the fireplace. How much did Brackston pay for her? She must have come from the west.

"What is your name?" he asked.

"Wa-ney." She never looked at him.

"You been here long?"

"No. Came last fall."

"How much did he pay for you?"

She shook her head. She did not understand the meaning of his words.

"How many horses did he give for you?"

She held up her fingers. Five.

"Take off your clothes. I want to see if you are worth five horses."

She did not move. He waited, containing his impatience. She would comply; she had no choice. At long last he watched her slowly straighten to her short height. Not looking at either of them, she bent forward and wiggled the leather dress off over her head. First her shapely legs shone in the firelight; then her small tight moon-shaped butt was exposed. Two small breasts shook underneath her. She pulled her head out of the dress, and her braids danced on her shoulders as she stripped the sleeves down her arms and stood up.

Black Wolf motioned for her to go to the bed. She closed her eyes, then marched to it. Carefully she put the dress on the ladder-back chair, and waited for his command with her back to him.

He moved behind her and felt her butt. Hard and muscled as he'd imagined it would be. His breath quickened as he fondled her breasts. They were small, but her nipples quickly stiffened under his palm. He felt himself growing harder while brushing the nipples on the center of his palms.

He used his toe to make her spread her legs apart. Then he pushed her head forward, forcing her to brace herself with her arms on the bed. His exploring fingers ran between her legs, and he grinned at the moisture he discovered with his fingertip. He probed her tight entrance and heard her sigh.

"Did that white men ever get his dick in you?" he asked, recalling the man's troubles with Pearlie.

She shook her head.

Black Wolf grinned. He could get his into her. He whipped aside the breechcloth and took his hard root in hand. Two steps forward and hard against her butt, he reached around and underneath her. With his fingers to open the way, he nosed his throbbing rod into her gates. Then he grasped her small waist and began to thrust himself into her.

At first it went slow, but soon her fluids and his hardness

won. She cried out to his pumping, and he almost laughed aloud. Brackston had never used her like this. He felt her contract inside. She gulped for more air.

He reached around and found her erection, above where he plunged in and out of her. With his index finger he massaged the hard button. Moans escaped her throat. She reached back and clutched his leg. Soon she sprawled facedown on the bed underneath him, groaning and crying out until at last she came and fainted under him.

Standing on his toes, he made a last drive to reach her deepest place, then emptied his seeds inside her belly. Groggy-headed and spent, he rose unsteady on his legs. He stripped the juicy slime from his still-hard shaft and wiped his hand on the blanket. She lay facedown, not moving. Black Wolf straightened and redressed himself.

Before he destroyed this place, he would give her the choice of blankets and anything else she wanted. With the animals in the corral, she could go home to her own people a rich woman. Drawn by her features, he carefully watched as she rose and got dressed. Her eyes avoided him. At last he knew and shook his head; he did not need another wife.

He went back to where Green Shirt sat cross-legged on the floor eating a piece of dog.

"Is it done already?" Black Wolf asked, taking a seat on the floor beside him.

"No, but you made me very hungry doing that to her."

Black Wolf nodded.

23

Slocum looked with concern at the ring of pink and purple predawn cresting the eastern horizon. Neither Blue Fox nor Black Wolf were back, and that worried him. Settlers had little respect for Indians. One of them might have shot the pair thinking they were on the warpath. He didn't dare leave the camp to Portugee John's care. The poor man would be drunk by ten o'clock, if he wasn't still that way from the night before.

He needed to go pay Mrs. Van Dam for another day's worth of her sweet hay. The animals were busy eating, no doubt in fear that they would soon have to leave the generous bunkers of forage. He planned to stay over at least for another day, unless she refused his money. Where was Black Wolf? They might have to stay longer if the two Sioux didn't show up.

Pearlie stood at the campfire, talking to Brad about a dress she planned to finish. Her words flowed so evenly and calmly one could almost imagine the garment. Blue Water had her busy stirring the kettle of boiling oats so they didn't burn or scorch.

"It'll be pretty when I get through with it," Pearlie said to Brad, and looked whimsically off into space.

"Why, I'll bet it will be the prettiest dress in all of Nebraska," Brad said, sipping his coffee.

"Maybe in the Dakotas too." She giggled and he laughed.

152

Slocum squatted down and poured himself a cup of coffee from the granite kettle. Blue Water joined him with a plate of freshly sliced bacon. She grinned privately at him over the way those two carried on. With nimble fingers, she gingerly placed the long strips into the hot skillet over the fire.

"Bacon and oats for breakfast," she announced for his approval.

"Sounds good to me," he said, and blew on his steaming coffee to cool it.

Red Deer joined him. The buck's long face told about his concern for the return of the others.

"You're worried too?" Slocum asked him.

"They gone for a long time."

"We'll give them today to come back." Slocum said. "Better check all the girths and strapping. It ought to warm up a little when the sun gets up and we should be able to repair all of it today. You hear that, Brad?"

"Yes, I did, sir. Fix and oil the harness too?"

"That's right. You will have to do Portugee John's too."

"I can do that."

"Good." He studied the early morning rays on the bluffs to the south of the Platte Valley. Where were those two? Had he lost them? It would be a long trip to Independence without their help. Dread hardened his concern. They had to come back unscathed.

Owl Woman began to hang everyone's blankets out to air. He frowned watching her. She spread them over the wagon wheels and on the corrals. Slocum wondered if she wanted something to do so she would not worry about her man's absence, or did she have a plan?

"Will those blankets work better doing that?" he asked when she came past him.

"If I had an anthill I would put them all on that," she said under her breath for only him to hear.

"Why?"

"A louse bit me last night."

He nodded, and took his coffee to where Blue Water stood with the long fork in hand to turn the bacon.

"She's freezing the bugs out of them," he said.

"Yes, she told me so earlier."

"Just checking," he said, and laughed.

At mid-morning, he and Blue Water went to see Mrs. Van Dam. She answered the door and invited them inside. Despite the dark interior of the cabin, he could see the once-fancy furniture and polished oak dining table. She seated them on ladder-back chairs at the fire.

"Mrs. Van Dam, we need to rest another day," he said when she took a seat and asked their business.

"I could let you stay another day for a dollar," she said.

"That's a fair price. If I may ask, what will you do out here alone?"

"I will manage, Mr. Slocum. This is all that I have now that the boys and their father are dead."

"But ranching—"

"Is man's work?"

"I meant—yes, I mean that."

"I can hitch and drive horses, mow, rake, and fix things. I'll hire a young man with a strong back to help me. I'm satisfied I can get along fine."

"We have a young boy on the train called Brad who lost his family to sickness. Someone stole everything they owned while he went for help to bury them. He might be interested in working for you when we come back from Independence."

"I would speak to him."

"He works hard—but he has been smitten by Pearlie."

"The nice young lady with the mind problem? Do you think he will marry her?"

Slocum looked at Blue Water but she shrugged. "We think he might. She has relatives in eastern Nebraska. We are taking her there for the Army. Outlaws killed her brother. The bad experience with them may have caused her mind to slip."

Slocum considered telling the woman that Jacks did it to her too, since he and his band had also attacked Mrs. Van Dam. But he worried how much the disclosure might upset the poor woman.

"Many worthless men on this frontier out here," she said. "That One-Eyed Jacks is the worst, but I guess there are others as bad."

"Yes, ma'am."

"This young lady can speak English very well, can't she?" the woman said, laying a hand on Blue Water's sleeve. "I would hope that you get her to teach the younger Indian children English as well as she speaks it."

"Be a good idea."

"Oh, it would be wonderful. But I wouldn't blame her if she didn't want to go back to that reservation."

"I better get back and check on things," he said, handing her the money in coin.

"Thank you. Mr Slocum. Speak to that boy for me about coming to work. I promise I won't mistreat him, and I like that mindless girl well enough—she would be some company. She could come too."

He thanked the lady. The two excused themselves and headed back for camp.

"You will leave when we come back?" Blue Water asked Slocum when they were outside the house.

He nodded. "Yes. There are men that search for me."

"You are no outlaw." She made a pained face at him.

"I am wanted by the law down in Kansas."

"But—"

"Blue. let's not worry about my leaving. We have much time to spend together."

"Yes. I wish we were alone now." She looked around as if seeking a place.

"We will have time for each other."

"Good."

Red Deer came running and pointing. "They come back! They come!"

Red Deer's eyes were better than his. Looking into the sun glaring off the snow to the south, Slocum could barely make out the far-off bluffs. He would have to accept Red Deer's knowledge and better vision. That he was right was all that mattered.

In another half hour, Black Wolf and Blue Fox wearily dropped from their horses in camp. Brad took their animals to water and feed. The two men had some new blankets with them. Slocum noticed that they gave them to the women.

He waited by the fire. Seated cross-legged, he let the radiant heat dance on his face and repaired a halter as he considered the Sioux chieftain's deliberate stride. Black Wolf dropped to his haunches across the fire and nodded with a satisfied look on his face.

"The trader who killed the boy is dead," he said.

Slocum saw the dark-brown scalp in his belt. He didn't need to ask more, merely nodded.

"It was the one with the hiders. Brackston."

"Good. When Portugee John is sober enough, I will tell him."

"Will he wish for the scalplock?"

"No." Slocum shook his head. He doubted the man was that much Sioux to want the bloody trophy. "Are Brackston's men about?"

"No, they must have stayed out there." Black Wolf motioned to the west.

"We will have to be very careful going back so we don't meet them."

"They will never know who killed him. They may even blame the poor Pawnee."

"The Pawnee are poor?" Slocum asked.

"They have eaten their horses."

Slocum could hardly believe Black Wolf's words, but agreed they must be very poor; he remembered their wonderful horses. Right after the war, he'd spent some time with a branch of the tribe in central Nebraska. They were handsome people, with lovely women, and their horses were the best bred in the world. They made the most powerful racers and came in many colors, including deep-colored paints with bald faces that could carry a man for miles at a hard run. All tribes prized them, and they often stole or tried to steal them. Many others came and traded for the animals, which were considered to have the greatest bloodlines on the plains.

"Ate all their horses?" Slocum asked in disbelief.

"The ones I spoke to had eaten theirs."

"We are repairing our gear today," he said, wondering why the Pawnee had done such a thing.

"Before I become like a Pawnee I will die," Black Wolf said.

Slocum only bobbed his head to indicate he had heard and understood Black Wolf's intentions. They could take his land, but not the man's dreams. If the Pawnees had eaten their horses, they had no dreams left.

24

They left Mrs Van Dam's ranch at dawn the following day. Earlier, Slocum had found Portugee John too drunk to even drive. He and Brad had physically loaded him in the back of the cart. The poor man had mumbled incoherently and waved at them. They'd covered him with blankets and paid him no mind.

"You drive the first one," Slocum said to the youth, and went to find Owl Woman. She could drive the second cart.

With a crunch of iron rims on the frozen snow, Brad led the procession toward the road. Owl Woman drove the second cart. Blue Water and Pearlie brought the string of rested ponies under their packs. The three Sioux came with the loose horses and helped herd the others. On their way at last, Slocum hoped they had no more delays.

If they didn't reach Independence and get headed back with the supplies, they might bog out of sight when the thaw came. He dreaded that more than anything. After a tight winter freeze, one warm rain and the entire countryside could turn into a quagmire. He hoped to be back to the Panhandle by then, if they didn't have any more problems. The notion made him shiver at the very thought of the horses bogging every step of the way to their knees and the wagons unable to move out of the sucking mud.

He glanced back at the long line. He'd better hurry along faster.

Black Wolf found the temperature warm and the days less harsh. Then a snow blew in one afternoon and made him hump up under his blankets. They spent three days of the storm with a German farmer. The animals ate his gray corn stalks from the bundles and yellow corn that he sold Slocum for twenty-five cents a bushel.

The farmer talked so differently, Black Wolf could not understand his broken English. One day he brought the chief a bowl of something that he wanted him to eat. The meat was in round cubes and the slick grass with it was bitter-tasting. Black Wolf recalled Slocum finding the same thing at the crazy woman's place in barrels.

"Sauerkraut!" the man said. "Very good."

"Yeah," Black Wolf said, not wanting to insult the man for Slocum's sake.

The farmer must have decided he really liked it, for the next day he came running through the snowstorm with more in a bowl for him.

"Sauerkraut," the German said.

"Sourkraut," Black Wolf said.

"Yeah. You know good what that is, huh?"

"Yes," Black Wolf said, and steeled himself to get ready to eat another bowl or risk making their host angry.

That evening in the blankets with Owl Woman, he belched out loud, and could retaste the peppery sausage flavor and the sourness of the fermented cabbage.

"Hmm, sourkraut. Be damn glad to get the hell away from that sourkraut."

She giggled. "He likes you."

"I don't like his sourkraut."

She rolled over and hugged him, laughing harder.

"Maybe I will make some for you one day," she offered.

He belched again, then squeezed her tight.

"Forget it. If I want some, I will come back and see him."

They both laughed, and she slipped underneath him.

"Maybe it makes him hard like you."

"I don't need it for that," he said, and moved over her silky legs. If he ever did need some for that purpose, he knew where this man lived, and he would come and trade for several barrels of it.

He eased himself into her. It was always good to make love with Owl Woman. Somehow she was the only one he simply enjoyed for the pleasure of it. He arched his back to go deeper into her. Slocum would be anxious to move on in the first light, if this snow quit. When Black Wolf reached back to keep the blankets from falling off them, he discovered the temperature outside their cocoon was dropping; the snow would stop by morning.

At dawn, Black Wolf was busy loading. The crust on the new snow was thin, and soon there came a regular storm of the loose powder swirling around them. Fine flakes landed on his face and the chill went deep. He managed to hang the heavy pannier on the horse on the first try, and then drew a deep breath. It would not be a pleasant day, but he had learned much about pack trains, and while they might make money for the men who worked them, the pay for the workers was not enough for all the labor they must do.

If he ever became a boss of one, then he could do it. Each day he learned more of the ways of Slocum. Past noon, Slocum rode back and invited him to go to the trading post in the next town. The adventure appealed to Black Wolf, more than swinging his quirt at lazy pack horses. Besides, he needed to look after Slocum. He handed the quirt to Blue Fox and rode off in a lope to join Slocum.

The small village sat in a low gap. Iron rims had churned the snow in the street into black crud. Many heads turned to study him. His eagle feather twisted over his shoulder in the wind. Look at me, I am a Sioux, he thought. I killed your brothers and sons at the Sweetwater Battle. Now I am one of you—look hard at me, white eyes. I am one of you now.

They reined up before the large store. He noticed how Slocum studied the situation and then dismounted. He did the same. When the big man went on the porch, he followed his lead.

Slocum's hand was on the door handle when a woman on

the porch began to scream. Black Wolf frowned at her. She dropped her parcels and threw her hands up in the air like a mad person, and her screeching was so loud it hurt his ears. He used his hands to cover them up.

"What's wrong with you?" Slocum demanded.

"He's a wild Indian!" she gasped.

"He's just an Indian, he isn't hurting you." A scowl formed on Slocum's face.

"Oh, but they are supposed to be on reservations, not out running around loose. Why, there is no telling what they will do."

By then a crowd of the curious had gathered. Black Wolf wondered if they would become a mob. So many whites, and only Slocum to stand up for him.

"How will they learn to be like us?" Slocum asked, restoring the packages to the woman's arms.

"Oh! They don't need to be here."

"Why not?"

A big man stepped forward. Black Wolf considered him a honyocker—a dirt farmer. He'd heard Slocum use the phrase before.

"The lady's right. The Army needs to keep them out there."

Black Wolf did not miss the low voices of approval by the others behind the big man. He wanted to say, "I am not a plower of grasses. Keep this land here that you have taken from the poor Pawnees and use your steel plows and plant corn on every bit of it if you like. I will stay far to the west and live with the buffalo. Don't come there. That is my land." But what would be the use of telling them? This fat woman who stood and berated him wanted him put under guard. She thought he might rape her.

Then he realized that Slocum was pulling him by the sleeve inside the store.

"We better get our things and get back," Slocum said in a voice that sounded concerned.

"Will it be like this in Independence?" Black Wolf asked, seeing the white people were still gathered on the porch.

"I hope not." Slocum scowled at the crowd outside.

"Good day, gentlemen, what do you need?"

"Two jugs of whiskey, box of matches, sack of salt, baking powder, some ginger, molasses ..." Slocum paused and glanced back toward the door.

Black Wolf could see the crowd was dispersing, but not without giving looks of hatred at the store. He knew they were intended for him. Slocum looked satisfied at their leaving, and after a deep breath, he went on listing the things he wanted from the clerk.

An abundance of smells new to Black Wolf filled the air inside the store—sweet, sour, and fresh aromas. Even at the fort he'd never seen so many things. Harness odors reminded him they still had ten days left to get to Independence.

He hoped his reception there would not be as harsh as at this place. Slocum handed him a long cigar. He tasted the end and the sweetness drew saliva from behind his teeth. It was too good to smoke. Maybe he would eat it like candy. Then the big man gave him some peppermint sticks, and he put the cigar away until later. They tasted even richer, and made his breath so fresh he wanted to puff on it.

Aside from the white woman and her "family," who, Slocum promised him, were not like all whites, he enjoyed his trip to the village. With sacks of goods tied over his lap, he rode the buffalo horse back with Slocum to where he'd told Brad to set up camp.

He must explain to Blue Fox and Red Deer about the dangers of white women and meeting them on the street. Those with big bellies like sows must be the worst kind. They should be avoided at any cost. The thinner ones shopping in the store never screamed at him. It was the big-bellied ones they must watch out for—not the pregnant ones. He could hardly wait to explain the differences in white women. He felt pleased with his discovery as he rode back in the warmer sun.

At this rate the snow would soon start to leave and the geese would wing north. They always came early, and he enjoyed a fat goose for supper. He would keep his eye out for the first sign of them.

25

From the creased envelope, Slocum studied the Army's instructions concerning Pearlie's known relatives. The town where her people lived was en route. He hoped he would find them willing to accept her. From his place beside the cart wheel he looked across the land surrounding their camp, and studied the fields of corn stubble poking out of the snow cover. Farms were closer and closer together here. There were more folks too.

The name of the village mentioned in the letter was Iron City. From what he had learned from their host farmer, it was less than a day's drive east of there. He pocketed the letter. What if there was no one to accept her? And would he lose Brad too if she left the train? The boy had good sense, but he was stuck on her. Slocum wished he had more answers. Surely in Independence he could hire some helpers to get the train back to Bordeaux.

"Slocum?" Brad called out, and hurried over.

"Yes?"

"I know Pearlie ain't—well, you know, but she's, well—" The youth sounded lost, but his sincerity showed through.

"Pearlie isn't your conventional person. Is that what you mean?"

"Yes," the youth said with some relief. "Do you think I could marry her?"

"Would she say yes to a preacher?"

"I think she would."

"Brad, she would always be a handful." Slocum shook his head slowly, considering all the problems Brad would face as her husband.

"I know that, but that Mrs Van Dam, she needs my help on her place, and she said she didn't mind Pearlie. Maybe we could live there and work for her when we get this train back."

"Right, but I don't know what Pearlie's relatives will think."

"What if they flat don't want her?"

"It's been worrying me too. That could be the case."

"We'll be there tomorrow and we should know how they feel. Won't we?"

Slocum agreed. The next day would bring the matter to a head. If they could find any Fountains. That was the name in the colonel's letter. Argile and Norma Fountain, Pearlie's uncle and aunt, were supposed to live near Iron City, Nebraska.

After they were stopped the next evening, Slocum promised Brad they would go into town in the morning and try to locate the Fountains. They camped along a frozen stream in a grove of trees, and found lots of wood. Slocum enjoyed the heat from the great campfire the women built as he wondered about the day ahead and Pearlie's fate.

The sparks burst skyward into the night. He felt the warmest he had been in ages. After supper, everyone looked content to sit, face the fire, and absorb the heat. Seated close by, Black Wolf nodded his approval of the big blaze. It was nice to have enough fuel to burn all one wanted to.

Following breakfast the next morning, the first place Slocum wanted to check on Pearlie's relatives was at the main store in the small town. Such places knew everything and everyone in the region, as well as where they lived. He and Brad rode past several wagon loads of yellow corn parked in the street. The lines were tied off, the brakes set with great Belgium or Clydesdale teams in harness that stood blowing vapor out their huge nostrils and stomping their great pie-sized hooves with impatience.

Slocum dismounted at the hitch rail before the largest mercantile on the street and handed Brad the reins.

"I will only be a moment and we should be on our way to finding them," Slocum said.

"I'll wait."

Slocum nodded and dodged the rack. He mounted the stairs and moved through the crowd of farmers. A bell rang when he opened the door, and the heat of the interior bathed his face. Smells assailed his nose. He excused himself to pass two ladies examining a pile of work shoes.

"I am looking for Argile Fountain. Do you know where he lives?" Slocum asked the gray-headed clerk at the counter.

The man made a displeased face at his question. "Sorry, mister, but the Fountains died of chol-erie just a month ago. Him and her both."

"Thanks." Slocum stepped back to allow a man to put some barn hinges on the countertop. Should he let the boy marry her? Why did he worry so? Pearlie had no one; Brad would treat her better than strangers. He went back outside, deeply engrossed in his concerns.

"What did you learn?" Brad asked, booting his pony closer and holding his reins to the bay out to him.

"We better find a preacher."

"Hurrah!"

Slocum waited to mount up. "You have to promise me one thing."

"What's that?"

"No honeymoon until this trip is over."

"What's that?"

"You and her can't sleep together until we get back to Fort Robinson."

The boy's face turned cherry red. "That's no problem."

"I'm sorry, but I think it will turn out better that way for the two of you."

Brad swallowed hard and bobbed his head in agreement.

They found a minister with the directions some farmers gave them. Reverend Thomas Larson, a little man with square glasses who looked afraid of his shadow, greeted them. He and his short, round-faced wife invited them inside their parlor.

Slocum stood, holding his cap against his leg, politely refusing the offer of a seat.

"Brad works for me. There is a young woman, an orphan, who he wants to marry. She's eighteen or twenty years old."

"A good age to get married." Larson nodded in agreement.

"Some bad things happened to her at the hands of outlaws and she, well, to be quite honest, Pearlie is some absent in her mind because of this. Brad here knows her well. He knows about her condition and wants to marry her." There, he had said it. Slocum drew a deep breath and studied the little man for his reply.

"If this young man is willing to accept this young lady's frailties in life, then who are we to say no?"

"Means—you'll marry us?" Brad stammered.

"Yes, of course."

"Could we do it in a few hours?" Slocum asked. "We have a large pack train and we're headed for Independence."

"I shall be here and ready," Larson said.

"And God bless you," his wife said, and patted Brad on the arm. "You are a true Christian marrying this poor girl."

"Yes, ma'am." Brad swallowed with difficulty.

The wedding party was made up of Blue Water, Owl Woman, Black Wolf, and Slocum. They all stood behind the pair. On their way back, they found a new calico dress that was perhaps a size larger than Pearlie needed, but in a pretty blue print. Blue Water and Owl Woman dressed her for the wedding in a bedroom at the parsonage. They both fussed over her.

Brad combed his hair with the part down the middle, and used some kind of rose oil on it. Slocum bought him a new shirt and pair of overalls so big around he needed galluses to hold them up—but Slocum knew they would shrink a lot in the first rain or washing.

Pearlie's light brown hair was braided tight and decorated with blue feathers. Her face was washed until it shined and she looked every bit the bride. Slocum felt a lump in his throat, standing back and wondering if all Brad's coaching would work on Pearlie. All she had to do was say yes.

The ceremony went fine. Pearlie stood there with him. She

even straightened Brad's collar once. Then Larson came to. "Do you, Pearlie Fountain, take this man, Brad Compton, to be your husband?"

The room fell deathly quiet. Slocum could hear the grandfather clock ticking in the hall. A floorboard creaked. Blue Water leaned forward and whispered in Pearlie's ear. A smile crossed the girl's lips and a light came on in her eyes.

"Yes, I do."

Brad drew a deep breath, and a look of relief swept both his and the little preacher's face.

"Then I pronounce you man and wife."

Slocum shouted, and Black Wolf did too. The women hugged Pearlie and danced around.

The little preacher took down his glasses and smiled.

Later, Slocum bought a fat heifer from a farmer for them to have red meat. The butchering process was completed in camp and the carcass hung in a tree to chill out. He could smell the fresh liver cooking in the skillet. Blue Water washed the blood from her hands and forearms.

"What did you say to her back at the wedding?" Slocum asked.

"I asked her did she think Brad was a nice young man."

"Good question and the right answer."

She smiled and winked at him. Had she really asked that, or something else? He'd never know. But it had worked. Mr. and Mrs. Compton—it would be okay. He wondered if the boy could keep his word about not having sex until they returned to Bordeaux's. He worried that having sex might make her worse. Her treatment in the hands of the outlaws had been what made her go crazy in the first place.

Portugee John, looking bleary-eyed, came from his cart. He was unsteady on his feet, and a cough seized him that doubled him over.

"They got married, huh?" he slurred.

"Yes, they did."

"Let's celebrate! Whoopee. I need some whiskey—"

"They don't have any here," Slocum lied. The man needed to dry out. He regretted buying the last two bottles. It was time for him to get over his losses. They'd driven his wagons and done his work long enough. His sorrow and his feeling sorry for himself needed to end.

"I've got to have some." The man sounded ready to cry.

"There isn't any and we aren't getting you any."

The man swung his arms around and searched the crew for someone to beg for a drink.

"Wolf-Wolf, you will get me whiskey?"

The chief shook his head.

"I got to have some whiskey—why, I'll die without it."

"No one's getting you any. From here on you better sober up," Slocum said.

"Can't. I got to have it—"

Portugee John's plight proved hard to watch. By morning, the poor man was almost shaking himself to death wrapped in two blankets. Slocum had warned everyone—nothing for him to drink. The man begged and pleaded for whiskey. The Indians avoided him. Brad even ceased being civil to him. They were within two days of Independence when they passed through a small village and somehow Portugee John managed to buy a small crock of whiskey.

Slocum caught him guzzling it down, jerked it away, and broke it on the wagon wheel. The shards of pottery and strong-smelling liquor flew everywhere.

"I hope you enjoyed it," Slocum said, and glared at the man. "That's all you are going to drink if I have to hog-tie you."

"You don't understand."

"Get in that cart and stay there." Slocum shoved him toward the tailgate.

"Brad!" Slocum shouted. "Get this thing moving." Portugee John clambered up and fell over inside the rig. "He's in!"

Still angry, Slocum started back down the line, untied his horse from the second cart, and nodded to Owl Woman, who sat on the seat. "Lets go."

"Plenty bad, huh?" she asked, meaning Portugee John.

"I'll dry him out," Slocum promised, and bounded on his horse.

Independence sat across the Missouri River on the bluffs. A jumble of buildings stretched down to the docks where riverboats were berthed. Slocum was grateful that the Chouteau warehouses were on the west bank, and thus he did not have to take his train over by ferry. The company had stables and forage for the horses.

A man named Jacques DeBloom showed them the cabin they could use while they were there, and also all the split wood piled outside for the fireplace. Slocum pointed the wood out to Blue Water and Owl Woman, and told them to go inside. Then he went back to supervise the unloading. He checked the bales off Jim's list, plus he had to look after Portugee John's business as well.

"Where did he go?" Slocum asked Black Wolf as the Chouteau men carried the last panniers inside. Under heavy overcast skies, he searched in the dim light—no sign of the man.

Black Wolf shook his head.

"That damn Portugee!"

"He is gone." Black Wolf shrugged off his disappearance. "He is a dead man. He will die soon."

"He wants to die. But he has to live. He has a woman, other children, a trading post."

"He is a dead man."

"Damnit, Black Wolf, I won't let him."

"You can't save him."

"You have seen this?"

Black Wolf nodded.

"There's nothing I can do to save him?"

"Nothing."

"I hear you. Hey, you over there. That's Mrs. Portugee's bales. Put them aside for her account." Slocum shut his eyes. He still had to go back and face her too. The hefty woman in the many-beaded dress. Damn, oh, damn. Life got tougher by the day. He had felt sorry for Portugee John having to tell her about their firstborn's death. Now Slocum had to tell her about both their deaths.

26

The authorities had no record of Portugee John's death, nor was he in jail with the drunks the police had gathered the night before. Concerned about the man's safety, Slocum checked on both sides of the river, and even DeBloom had no idea where else to look when all his inquiries about the man turned up nothing. Slocum could not believe the man had merely walked off and disappeared on the first dreary day when they'd reached town.

Snow mixed itself with rain. It dripped off the eaves when he returned. The cabin was a welcome shelter after his disappointing day. The building contained several bunk rooms and a large main room with a long rough table and benches to seat an army. Well-chinked walls and the fire in the large fireplace raised the temperature inside to toasty.

"Didn't find him," he said, removing his wrap and coat.

"I have some hot coffee," Blue Water said, and brought him a freshly poured cup.

"Where is everyone?" he asked, looking around. Red Deer and Blue Fox sat at the table, but no one else was in sight.

"Tired, I guess, and went to bed," she said, but did not look at him.

"So early?"

She held her finger to her lips to silence him. "I have food cooked."

He glanced down the hallway. Those others must be back in there. Black Wolf and Owl Woman—Brad and his bride. His concerns for Pearlie must have been unfounded.

"Sounds quiet to me," he said. "You think they know how?"

"Yes." She gave him a perturbed look.

"What's to eat?" He decided his teasing would only make her mad.

"Beef. Chouteau's man brought us potatoes."

"You did good."

"And he also brought some fresh bread just from the oven, he said, and butter too."

"Sounds wonderful. You two ate yet?"

Red Deer patted his belly. "Ate too much."

Blue Fox agreed. "Plenty full. Good food."

"I saw a tub outside. I think right after supper I am going to take me a hot bath." Slocum took a seat at the table by the other two.

"Is that what white men do? Take baths in winter?" she asked, delivering several large cuts of brown meat on a wooden slab. Then she returned with several steaming small potatoes in a bowl. He took out his skinning knife to cut the fresh French bread. The thought of the tasty meal flooded his mouth with saliva.

"Yes," he said, whittling off slices from the long loaf. "It ain't bad either to get all the horse-sweat smell and dirt off of you, at least for a while."

She nodded.

After he ate, he set up the tub in their room. She bathed first and then rushed to climb in bed and get under the covers. He did the same thing right after her. The bunk proved to be narrow, but they managed to squeeze into it. Filled with the excitement of being clean and having their first privacy in weeks, they soon made love.

"When will we go back?" she asked him afterwards, snuggled against his chest.

"Day after tomorrow. We are running out of time. A warm rain and we would be another month getting back for the mud. You think Pearlie understood tonight?" he asked.

"Yes. She trusted him."

"Good. What do you want from this place?"

"Nothing but you."

"No, I mean store things. Material to make a dress? Jewelry?"

"I would like a blue dress like hers."

"You will have it."

Blue Water giggled and nuzzled her face in his chest. "You are a good man, Slocum. My bed will be empty when you go away."

"I have not gone yet."

"No."

He would have to—someday, but not yet.

In the morning he saddled his horse and rode to the ferry. He found the blue-checkered dress in a small shop in the business district over in Independence, and the lady offered to fit it for his wife, but he said she was too far away to come and have that done. Then he stopped and bought a large sack of hard candy for everyone before he headed back.

"The man wants to see you up at the office," Blue Water said when he returned.

"Good. Perhaps he has some good news of the Portugee." He handed her the package and hugged her tight. "Go try it on. I will be right back." He showed the candy bag to the others and put it on the table. "Here are some sweets. Help yourselves."

"What is this?" she asked, staying close to him with the package.

"Your blue dress. Go try it on." He gave her a small shove. "I will be right back."

He entered the warehouse office, and at the sight of him, Jacques came hurrying to the front. The man looked very concerned, and Slocum wondered what was wrong.

"*Monsieur,* I have word there are bounty hunters in town looking for you."

"The Abbott brothers?"

"*Oui.* That is the name I heard."

"I'll head west. You help get the train loaded in the morning. Be sure they have all the things Jim Bordeaux ordered and help them get out the gate."

"Who will be in charge?" The man frowned at his instructions.

"Black Wolf can handle it. He knows the way back. The boy, Brad, can handle the rest."

"What will you do?"

"Just go. Spread the word I am riding to Santa Fe."

"Take this." Jacques handed him a small crucifix. "If you are ever at one of our trading posts, show them that and they will take care of you. You are one of us. No one else could have gotten this train here this time of year. You sure the chief can get them back?" He narrowed his eyes with concern.

"Yes."

"Good luck, and I am glad I met you, Slocum."

"My pleasure." He pocketed the crucifix and shook the man's hand.

Back at the cabin, he gave his instructions to all of them. Black Wolf would lead the way back. Brad would do the negotiating and trading for the train. The youth could make the deals to camp each night since some of the white farmers might not let Indians stay overnight on their places.

"Where will you go?" Brad asked.

"I hope to rejoin you later when they're gone. But we must not say a word of that. I want them to think I went to Santa Fe."

"So do we," Black Wolf said solemnly.

Slocum would have sworn the chief wanted to say more, but hesitated. He hated to part company with them. Even Pearlie, quiet for once, acted taken aback by his announcement.

"I will pack you some food," Blue Water said, and rushed about in her new dress.

Slocum began to roll up the new blankets for a bedroll in the canvas sheet he'd bought from Jacques's stock. Blue Water would need all of their covers. Winter was far from being over.

"Not too fast or too slow," he said to Black Wolf.

"Watch the horses' backs. We won't have many extras," the chief said, mimicking Slocum's words at Bordeaux's the first day.

"We did it right."

"Yes. I will too. You know you can come live in my camp.

She will be there." Black Wolf nodded toward Blue Water.

"I know, and if they leave, I will rejoin you. Hang a red flag up if you think or know they're close by."

"We will do that."

"Black Wolf?"

"Yes?"

"You don't have to kill them for me."

He nodded.

Slocum hugged and kissed Blue Water good-bye. Then he held her at arm's length and gazed at her new blue dress. He hugged her a last time, then went outside and tied his bedroll on behind his saddle. Blue Fox brought him the Winchester and he slid it in the scabbard. Then he turned to face Blue Water. She stood straight-backed, wrapped in a blanket. Flakes of light sleet fell on her face and hair.

"Will you ever come to Red Cloud's reservation and see me?" she asked.

"I will try."

"My lodge will be there."

"I have money coming for making this trip. Bordeaux will pay that to you."

"I don't need it."

"Of course you need it."

Black Wolf said that he would handle the matter. Slocum thanked him and kissed her good-bye again. His heart was not in leaving, but he knew he must or risk others getting hurt. At last, he mounted his horse and with a wave rode out of Chouteau's compound into the night.

Black Wolf watched him leave. Was that what the Great Spirit Woman of the Sioux wanted him to do? Let Slocum ride away? He still had not learned about his people's future. Even the rifles that Bordeaux had promised him were still in their crates. He must rely on this boy Brad to find them places to camp. And he knew they would travel among people who hated Indians. It would take much powerful medicine for him to guide this train back. He remembered the trail they'd come on, but now he must retrace it without Slocum.

He shut his eyes to all the things he needed do. This was

much worse than going to rob horses from the Crow. Then he'd only had to worry about his own horse and armaments, not an entire train. He would be very busy with this task; his belly hurt thinking about it. He must use the white man's ways going home.

They left Independence at daybreak the next day. He felt grateful the sky had cleared. Jacques warned Black Wolf to watch for the Abbott brothers. The pair had been around asking about Slocum. The older and heavier-built one, Lyle Abbott, rode a big Appaloosa horse with a blanket of black spots.

Black Wolf agreed to watch out for them. He carried his oily new Winchester, fresh from the crate, in a boot on his saddle. It was loaded with fresh brass .44/40 cartridges to the gate. With a new unblocked hat on his head that Jacques had given to each of the four men, Black Wolf waved for Brad to drive the first cart out into the street. The big draft horse, filled with new energy from his three days' rest and good feed, stomped out and started north. Even the pack ponies danced a little with excitement under their packs of trade goods.

Headed home at last. He did not want to live among so many people. There must be thousands there. He could not count all that went by the compound each day. Many did not look like they would make soldiers, but there were more whites than he'd counted passing on the trail. The thoughts of their numbers did not making him think lightly of the white man. They had more men than he'd ever dreamed were in the world.

Black Wolf huddled under his blanket on his buffalo horse and set the pace in front, winding up the street. They were going home with enough repeating rifles and ammunition for each of his men. The cold did not feel nearly as biting. Somehow he must do this thing, take the pack train back. He hoped he had Slocum's ability to lead them.

They camped that evening with a farmer they'd stayed with before. He accepted fifty cents for his hay and feed and asked the boy about Slocum. The youth told him Slocum had been delayed and would join them later. The farmer nodded and accepted the coins Brad paid him.

"Come back anytime," he said, and hurried off to the small sod house.

Black Wolf wondered if he could ever sleep in such a house. The cabin back at Chouteau's wasn't bad. He had a new crosscut saw and file of his own in the cart. Maybe he and Owl Woman would build one for the wintertime. But that would mean he would have to stay there forever. Perhaps he would consider more about the matter of a house later.

"Someone is coming on horses," Brad pointed out.

"It is them." Black Wolf rushed for his Winchester on the saddle.

"Remember, he said not to kill them," Brad said, hurrying to keep up with him.

"I want to be sure they don't kill us."

They rode in. The swarthy-faced one rode a dark Appaloosa horse with a white blanket rump and big black spots. The younger man, equally bearded, rode a chestnut horse and reined up beside his brother.

"We're looking for John Slocum," the big man said.

Wolf cradled the Winchester in his arms. "No one here by that name."

"We got it on good word this is his pack train."

"Someone lied to you, mister," Brad said. "This train belongs to Jim Bordeaux. Black Wolf here is the ramrod."

"Black Wolf, huh?" Abbott scowled. "I'm going to look around."

"You are going die too," Black Wolf said. He thumbed back the Winchester's hammer in a loud audible snap.

"Hold up there, Injun. I'm the law here in Kansas. I can take you in."

"Not dead you can't."

"You threatening a peace officer?"

"No. You ride past me you will be dead."

"You hiding that damn Slocum in there?"

"He's not here."

"Ferd, I reckon we'll just go get us a warrant and arrest the whole gawdamn bunch of them."

"Hey," Black Wolf said, and caused Lyle to rein his horse back.

"You better have a grave dug, you come back here."

"Why?"

" 'Cause I ain't burying your dead carcass."

"Come on, we'll get us a warrant." Lyle booted the big Appaloosa away.

"What're we going to do now?" Brad asked him.

Black Wolf shook his head as he watched them throw up mushy snow in their wake. Had his anger caused them to go for more help? He wished Slocum had stayed. He would know what to do.

"They won't be able to use Kansas law on us," Brad said, "if we hurry and get to Nebraska, but it's a ways up there to the line."

"Load up!" Black Wolf shouted, and caused the others to look his direction in surprise. "We go to Nebraska now!"

All the horses' heads were down and snorting powdery snow from the long push and no rest. They'd been on the road over a full day and night. Slocum would have disapproved of such a long drive, but the boy had repeatedly promised Black Wolf that those men's Kansas law would not hold in Nebraska. Black Wolf looked back to the south and saw no sign of pursuit. He hoped the boy knew what he was talking about. In the gray light of dawn, Brad rode off down a lane to talk to a farmer about feeding their stock and them staying there to rest.

In a short while the youth returned.

"He says yes, we can stay here and we are in Nebraska."

Black Wolf nodded. Maybe this would work. He hoped the horses would recover so they could go at the next sunrise. Somewhere a shrill rooster crowded. Black Wolf wondered where Slocum was.

27

Black Wolf led the train westward beyond the crowded farms, into the more open prairie along the Platte. Temperatures warmed each day, and Brad was forced to drive the cart where the larger wagons had not broken through the ruts. Crossing small streams that fed into the Platte became more dangerous, and in some the ice had broken away. They were forced to wade across these, using the two big horses on one cart and then going back for the other one.

In over a week, Black Wolf had not seen the Abbott brothers. He felt they were simply not showing themselves, spying on his train, hoping to surprise Slocum. Once he thought he saw a flash of light from the lens of a telescope, but no sign of them or Slocum. He kept the red flag waving on a strong branch attached to the front cart.

They camped for the night close by the river. Blue Fox pointed out to him the slush and water on top of the Platte's surface near where he chopped a hole in the ice for the horses to drink. Black Wolf agreed; the thaw was close. They needed to be further west, where he hoped there would less mud. If only he could make them go faster, but he knew they were already stretching the days into long miles. Being a white man was not as easy as he'd thought it would be.

He started past where Blue Water was standing. Then he

paused and noticed how weary she appeared as she searched hard in the direction they'd come from.

"Do you see him?" he asked her in Sioux.

"No, but I fear those men found him and that is why we have not seen them."

"No, they don't have him."

"You know that?"

He nodded. Had he told her a lie? No, he believed that Slocum would join them when he felt it was safe. Black Wolf went on and found the other men sitting at the campfire. They looked dog-tired, as did both of the women there. Perhaps he should rest them for a day. No, they needed to be further west when the thaw came.

"At the woman's place we will rest for a day," he told them in English.

"Good," Brad said, and shook his head wearily. Blue Fox and Red Deer, who looked equally exhausted, acknowledged his words.

The second evening they reached the Van Dam claim. Even the big Belgium horse Brad drove hung his head down. The widow came out to meet them.

"Where is Slocum?' she asked when the youth reined up.

"He had some problem. He's coming later. Black Wolf is in charge. Can we stay a day or so?"

"Why, of course. You all look completely worn out. There you are, Pearlie, my dear."

"We are tired, ma'am. We really are," Brad mumbled.

Pearlie dismounted and ran to hug her. Black Wolf watched the two women busy talking, then turned in the saddle and looked back east. Still no sign of the Abbotts or Slocum. In a week they would be home, and he would be glad to be there.

The packhorses were too tired to even eat the sweet hay they fed them in the bunks. Hip-shot, they slept on their feet. Black Wolf worried that he had gone too far too fast and the animals wouldn't be able to make the last 150 miles or so back to the reservation. When he returned to camp, the others were all ready crawling into bedrolls, going to sleep though the sun was not yet down.

Perhaps they would stay over for two days. He would feed

the ponies well each day and then they would be ready to go on. It was lucky none had turned up lame and their backs were not raw. He would remember what Slocum had taught him. He only wished the man was there.

He had not had time to seek the Great Spirit and find out what he must do next. Maybe he should go gather some sagebrush and make a fire away from camp. If she came—would she tell him the future of his people?

What should he do for them? Would the rifles save his people? They would all be armed with the new repeaters. Many things he did not know. There were questions only the Great Spirit could answer.

He rode off by himself on his buffalo horse and built the fire on the ridge. Seated on the robe he carried with him, he fed the tough twisted branches on the flames. Much of the snow was gone, leaving the brown grass only spotted with remaining patches. Still, the evening wind was sharp and carried his smoke away. He sat under the blanket and prayed for the Great Spirit to return and tell him his future.

Sunset and darkness settled on the land. Alone, he listened to the wolves howl at the crescent moon. No vision came, and hours later Black Wolf remounted his horse and rode back to camp. He unsaddled and crawled under the covers with Owl Woman.

"You had no food. You want some?" she asked.

"No. I will sleep."

"No vision?"

"No vision."

Slocum pushed the bay horse closer. At last he dismounted and went the last quarter mile on foot. He was about to run out of moonlight. The crescent hung low and he had only a half hour left to see by it. The bitter smell of wood smoke reached his nose. Then he heard a sleeping horse grunt in the night—good, he had found their camp. Through the trees he could see the fire had burned low enough. They must be asleep. He untied the two horses from the picket line and led them back through the trees, listening closely for any sounds of alarm.

He remounted the bay and set out northward at a lope. The Abbott brothers were afoot and would be a day or so getting their horses back.

At sunup the following morning in a small nearby farming community, he left their horses with a sleepy-eyed flunky for the wagon yard.

"Here's a half-dollar for their keep. They'll be coming after them. Yes, and their name's Abbott." First, though, the brothers would have to track him through the snow. He had not made that easy. With a slow grin on his face, Slocum rode out of town.

He short-loped the bay westward. In half a day he arrived at the Van Dam place. The two Indian women were busy washing clothes. Pearlie rushed out to greet him.

"And we been worrying about you," she said, clutching his arm. "You been gone so long. And you know, we're going to live here? Brad and me."

"That's wonderful," he said, looking past her into the excited brown eyes of Blue Water, who came stripping her arms of suds and running as fast as she could to get to him.

"Excuse me, Pearlie," he said, and took Blue Water in his arms.

"I was worried."

"Don't ever worry about me." He held her head to his chest. Then he frowned. Four riders were coming around the plum thicket and out of the draw straight towards them. He recognized the front rider—it was One-Eyed Jacks.

"Black Wolf, the outlaws are coming!" he shouted, and tried to push her back so he could draw his Colt. The four men were bearing down on him.

Too late. He saw Jacks's gun smoke, and felt the bullet slap into her back. He caught her, and tried to remove his Colt and return their fire. Pearlie screamed beside him.

Mrs. Van Dam rushed out of the house with a shotgun. Her first blast cut Jacks off his horse. The other riders divided and turned around. Her second barrel of buckshot hit one of the rider's horses in the rump, and he went to bucking and ducked his tail up between his butt. He soon pitched his rider. Their rifle fire sent him send racing away. The downed rider rose to his feet blazing away at them with a Colt, and was cut down by the .44/40's. Then the last of the outlaws disappeared from view on horseback.

In a minute, both Blue Fox and Red Deer were on their own horses charging after the outlaws with their new long guns. Slocum held Blue Water's limp body, desperate to save her. A knot rose in his throat; the Colt fell from his fingers.

The cold, stark realization hit him; any effort to save her would be futile. Her life slipped away. Warm blood soaked his hand and arm beneath her. Owl Woman spread out a blanket for him to put her on, and he knelt in the slush to place her gently on it.

Then a small whisper came from her lips. "I did see you in—the water."

"Yes, I believe you," he said in a dry whisper.

And she died.

•

28

On the first day of the chokecherry moon, Slocum arrived at Bordeaux's trading post.

"I thought you'd be back in Texas by now," the trader said, coming outside to shake his hand. "After you brought the pack train back, you sure made yourself scarce around here."

"I'm on my way to Texas right now. Had a little business in Deadwood to attend to first."

"Gold or cards?"

"Both. How's Jeanne?"

"There she is. Ask her yourself. You two go inside, I'll put your horse in the corral."

The dark-haired woman rushed out from the dugout doorway and hugged him. Then she leaned back in his embrace and looked up hard at him.

"What! You are not sick and come to see me?"

"Fit as a fiddle. How's the Sioux? I don't see anyone around their camp. Where are they?"

"It is head-count day. That Captain Brown, he has not forgiven Black Wolf for getting the pass either. There are many bad words passed between them."

"Maybe I need to go see about it?"

"Oh, he will not listen."

"Brown or Black Wolf?"

"Neither of them. They are hardheaded as goats."

"Hey, leave that saddle on," he said to Jim. "I'm going to that head count.

"Be back to visit in a little while." He tightened the girth and mounted up. With a polite nod to them, he set the horse into a lope. He figured the head count must be taking place further west along the small stream.

Atop the ridge, he made out two companies of troopers who were dismounted. An Army ambulance with a new white tarp over the bows was parked at the end of the formation. Slocum considered the formation of soldiers and the handlers holding the horses. They seemed much too hostile if they were only there for a head count.

He rode around the wagon, glanced inside the partially opened end, and stopped short. Set up in the bed behind the canvas sheet was one of the latest Gatling guns on a tripod, pointed at the many Indians gathered in the creek bottom near the table.

"Get back," some sergeant shouted at him.

Slocum never heeded the man's words. He set spurs to the bay.

"Black Wolf! It's a trap!" he shouted, and lashed the bay forward. He drew his own pistol, and the three officers talking to the Indian leaders turned with looks of dismay on their faces.

"Brown, call off your dogs!" Slocum shouted.

"This is an outrage! Disarm that man!" Brown shouted to his subordinates.

No one moved to obey. Slocum dismounted by kicking his leg over the saddlehorn, landed on his feet, and held the pistol at arm's length pointed at the man's heart. "Anyone makes a move, you're dead, Captain."

"You will be hung for treason for this!" Brown said loud enough that the troopers on the rise could hear him.

"You, sir, will be tried for attempted murder of these Indians." Slocum looked at the next officer. "You, Lieutenant, get on your horse and bring Colonel Wilton out here at once."

"But, sir—" The young officer looked lost as to what to do.

"You make one move for this man, Lieutenant, and you'll be court-martialed with him!" Brown shouted.

"You don't go get the colonel, Lieutenant, you're going to be in this with him. Murdering Indians is not the Army's duty out here." Slocum wondered how long he could hold this dead-man's hand.

"I'll go," the lieutenant said, and rushed off for his horse.

"You bastard, you! You had to come back here. You had to spoil this!" Brown's face grew purple with rage. He clenched his fists at the sides of his legs. "I'll have all of you in irons. Do you hear me? Do you hear me? I'd have killed them to the last one like they did to Custer. I'd have killed them to the last one!"

The wind carried his words away. No one moved. Slocum knew the others would wait for the colonel, and holstered his revolver. The Indians began to sit down on the ground. Black Wolf came over and put his hand on Slocum's shoulder.

"I am glad to see you, my friend. I have seen brave men before, but never this brave. They could have shot you."

"He would have shot you and all of the others if I hadn't stopped him."

Black Wolf nodded and looked to the north. The Great Spirit had said he would save them. Now he finally knew how.

"Where will you go?" He turned around to speak to Slocum. "Are those two men still looking for you?"

"They always will look for me." Slocum shook his head to dismiss the man's concern. "When this is over I'm going back to Texas and get warm."

"I will ask the Great Spirit of the Sioux to watch after you on your journey."

"Yes, I'll need her too," Slocum said, and listened to the wind snap the fresh canvas on the wagon's bows. He was thinking about the cantinas and the music, but it would be many moons before he would ever forget about Blue Water.

JAKE LOGAN
TODAY'S HOTTEST ACTION WESTERN!

LONGARM

Explore the exciting Old West with one of the men who made it wild!

J. R. ROBERTS
THE GUNSMITH